SHAMELESS WITH HIM

A Less Than Novel

CARRIE ANN RYAN

Shameless With Him
A Less Than Novel
By: Carrie Ann Ryan
© 2020 Carrie Ann Ryan
ISBN: 978-1-947007-81-9

Cover Art by Charity Hendry
Photograph by Wander Photography

Praise for Carrie Ann Ryan

"Carrie Ann Ryan knows how to pull your heartstrings and make your pulse pound! Her wonderful Redwood Pack series will draw you in and keep you reading long into the night. I can't wait to see what comes next with the new generation, the Talons. Keep them coming, Carrie Ann!" –Lara Adrian, New York Times bestselling author of CRAVE THE NIGHT

"Carrie Ann Ryan never fails to draw readers in with passion, raw sensuality, and characters that pop off the page. Any book by Carrie Ann is an absolute treat." – New York Times Bestselling Author J. Kenner

"With snarky humor, sizzling love scenes, and brilliant, imaginative worldbuilding, The Dante's Circle series reads as if Carrie Ann Ryan peeked at my personal wish list!" - NYT Bestselling Author, Larissa Ione

"Carrie Ann Ryan writes sexy shifters in a world full of passionate happily-ever-afters." – *New York Times* Bestselling Author Vivian Arend

"Carrie Ann's books are sexy with characters you can't help but love from page one. They are heat and heart blended to perfection." *New York Times* Bestselling Author Jayne Rylon

Carrie Ann Ryan's books are wickedly funny and deliciously hot, with plenty of twists to keep you guessing. They'll keep you up all night!" USA Today Bestselling Author Cari Quinn

"Once again, Carrie Ann Ryan knocks the Dante's Circle series out of the park. The queen of hot, sexy, enthralling paranormal romance, Carrie Ann is an author not to miss!" *New York Times* bestselling Author Marie Harte

To J.

Thanks for being my friend in every country we met. And for making such an impression I just had to write you into a book.

Shameless With Him

New York Times and USA Today bestselling author Carrie Ann Ryan completes a sexy contemporary series with an unrequited crush on the bad boy next door.

Caleb Carr might have once been ready for commitment, but when the unexpected slams into him with the force of a two-ton truck, he knows he has to run away from anything that might be important. Zoey might well be his final temptation, but to keep her whole, he'll walk away.

Zoey Wager has loved Caleb since they were eight. And has had her heart broken from afar repeatedly ever since. It doesn't help that every time she sees him—even when she's running away halfway across the world—he's with another woman. She's watched him fall in lust her entire life. Now, she's ready to watch him fall in love. With her.

Shameless With Him

A LESS THAN NOVEL

By
Carrie Ann Ryan

Chapter 1

Zoey

ZOEY & CALEB – AGE 8

Hawaii was *everything*. I mean, where else on Earth could you wear a grass skirt *and* go to a pig roast, where they gave you pretty flowers to wear? I loved it here, and I never wanted to go home.

We'd been in Hawaii for four days, and I knew we needed to go to the airport tomorrow. I didn't care. All I wanted to do was play in the sand and the waves today, and my mom was finally letting me do it. We'd had to stay away from the beach for most of the trip because Lacey hadn't been feeling well, even though the doctors said the cancer was gone.

I rubbed my hip, remembering the big needle that

had made me throw up. My mom said I wouldn't have a scar from giving my little sister my bone marrow, and I didn't know if she'd lied to me or not. She lied to me lots of times, though. Like when she said it wouldn't hurt. And that Lacey would get all better because I had to go through the procedure, too.

It had taken Lacey forever to get better, and my mom still watched her every move and wouldn't let me do fun things because she was afraid I'd get hurt, too. Sometimes, I thought Mom only cared about me because I could help Lacey, then I remembered the times it was just *our* time and no one else's. When we'd plant flowers and then put together pretty vases with the flowers we cut later.

Mom was up in the room with Lacey now. Today was all about me and Dad. We wouldn't stay long since I didn't want them to be sad they weren't outside, but for now, I got to play in the waves. *Finally.*

Sand tickled my feet, and I looked over at Daddy.

"Having fun, Z-baby?"

I smiled wide. I wasn't a baby, Lacey was the baby. Though I liked being Daddy's baby sometimes. "I love it. Thank you."

He looked sad for a moment, then he smiled back at me before he turned and jumped into a wave. I laughed. I loved swimming and followed him into the ocean, letting the waves slap into my back, trying not to drink too much salty water.

There were other kids around us, all of them laughing and playing with each other rather than their families. I wanted this time with Daddy.

Then someone slammed into my back, and I slipped. Sand smacked into my face, and water surrounded me. I twisted and turned, trying to get up. I couldn't find the top of the water. My heart beat fast, and I tried to put my feet on the ground. I didn't know where it was.

Before I could scream or think about anything other than the burn in my eyes, hands were on my shoulders, lifting me up. I coughed and sputtered, trying to wipe at my face. Another wave hit me, but the hands never let go.

"Are you okay? Wait. Zoey?"

I blinked away the saltwater and looked into the eyes of Caleb Carr. *Caleb?* "What are you doing here?" I blurted.

"Rescuing you, of course. I didn't know your family was going to be in Hawaii, too."

Caleb went to school with me, and I loved him. Not that I'd ever say that out loud. I totally loved him and knew that one day I would marry him. He was everything I loved in a boy. With that sweet smile, big, blue eyes, and hair he always flipped back that made him look *so* cool. Once, he'd even shaved the sides to make a kind of mohawk. The teachers weren't happy, though Caleb and his family hadn't cared. I'd loved it, because I'd loved him then, too.

Now, this was officially the most perfect vacation ever. I had the ocean, sand, and Caleb Carr.

"We came because Lacey isn't sick anymore."

Caleb's mouth turned down a bit in a frown, and I wanted to kick myself for bringing up Lacey. No one liked talking about sick kids, even if you *were* a kid. Caleb let go of my shoulders as the waves slapped into our sides.

"I'm glad." He paused. "Anyway, sorry that Laura almost drowned you. She screamed when she saw a fish and hit you."

"Laura?"

He nodded towards the shore, and I looked over at the girl in the pretty pink bathing suit currently staring at me and Caleb like I was evil.

"She's here on vacation, too. She's from England." Caleb's mouth tipped up in a little smile that I hated.

Hated it because it wasn't for me.

No, it was for some girl named Laura.

"Zoey? Are you okay? Damn it, Zoey, don't go off with strangers." Daddy pulled me towards him and away from Caleb, and it was all I could do to keep from blushing. As Laura waved at Caleb from the shore, and he nodded at me before going to her, I told myself I was okay. Just fine.

I wasn't.

Because today was only the first time Caleb Carr would fall for someone who wasn't me. I knew it deep down in my heart, I knew this wouldn't be the last.

ZOEY & Caleb – Age 15

I wasn't sure I was a fan of camping. However, I was a fan of s'mores. I bit into the chocolatey gooey mess and moaned around the graham cracker.

"Good?" Dad asked.

I nodded, taking my final bite before going about licking my fingers one by one. There was no point in wasting the goodness with a napkin just yet.

"Want another?"

I shook my head before taking a sip of my soda so I could wash down the deliciousness. "I'm good. Any more sugar, and I'll probably end up having to roll myself down to the lake later for the show."

"There's going to be music, right? I love music." Lacey leaned into my shoulder, and I shifted so she could have more room. She wiggled a bit and sighed as she nuzzled into my side.

"That's what the director said when we checked into

the campsite," Mom answered, looking down at her folder that never seemed to leave her side, not even when we were hiking in the woods for most of the day. If there was something to plan, schedule, or fix, my mom would have it color-coded within the hour. Dad said she'd always been that way but had gotten even more so when Lacey was sick.

Now, my sister was better—I crossed my fingers even as the thought flitted across my mind—and Mom was just as detail-oriented as ever. The fact that she was doing her best to use those skills to help me get into the best colleges even though I was only a sophomore might be nice, except it also stressed me out, so I wasn't going to think about it too much.

We watched the flames for a bit longer, then after Dad had doused the campfire, we headed down for the show as a family. It was nice for it to be the four of us since, most of the time, we didn't have the time to hang out and just *be*.

"Mom, can we sit over there?" Lacey asked, tugging on Mom's sleeve and stepping in front of me at the same time. I didn't mind since I had my eyes on something— no, *someone*—in the distance.

"Sure, honey," Mom said, looking over at me, though I couldn't really focus on her words. "Zoey?"

I blinked, tearing my gaze from the shadowy figure across the way near the lake, the one that couldn't be real because I couldn't be that unlucky.

"I'm going down there, okay? I think I see someone from school."

"Mom," Lacey whined, clearly tired from the day. I didn't blame her. We'd been going full-speed all day, and she didn't have the best stamina. "We're going to miss those seats and the best view."

"Okay, okay." Mom looked at me. "Be safe, and only ten minutes, all right? You understand me?"

I nodded, a little surprised that she was letting me go off alone. Of course, there were adults all around, and this particular campsite was filled with people from our neighborhood since this was a planned trip. Mom knew practically everyone here, so I was sure she felt confident that there would always be eagle eyes on me.

I kept going to where I had seen the shadow, my heart racing. I did my best to discreetly wipe my mouth, hoping I didn't have chocolate on my face.

"Zoey-girl?" Caleb Carr asked, coming out of the shadows. He had a wide grin on his face, and his eyes were dark. That lock of his hair that always fell over his eyes did wonderful things to my stomach.

Every time I was near Caleb, I lost the ability to speak. I couldn't help it. He just did things to me. Plus, he called me *Zoey-girl*. It wasn't too original. Nevertheless, it was a nickname. That meant he knew me. He *saw* me. It totally counted as *everything*. Right?

"Hi, Caleb. I didn't know your family was here."

He nodded. "Dimitri is even here somewhere. Drinking beer since he's allowed to now."

"Really?" I asked, trying to keep my heart in check.

"Yep. He turned twenty-one and is lording it over us." Caleb just shrugged. "Well, mostly Devin since he's closer to that age. You know?"

"At least you'll reach that before Amelia does," I said, mentioning his younger sister.

"She'll be last at everything. Though she'll always gripe about it." He shrugged. "How's Lacey doing?"

He asked the question because he knew what we'd gone through. He didn't have pity in his voice like so many others, though. And that was just one more reason I loved him.

Argh.

"She's doing great. She's here." I gestured vaguely over my shoulder to where my family was. I couldn't keep my eyes off of him, though, so I hoped I was facing the right way.

"Good. I'm glad you guys are all here. I know you haven't been able to do this every year with the rest of the neighborhood."

I warmed all over, my mouth ready to say something, *anything*. Only as soon as I parted my lips, another voice filled the air.

"Caleb." A giggle. Then an arm slid around Caleb's trim waist, and a slender hand slipped into his front pocket. He looked down. Amber, the gorgeous honor roll student in our class with the perfect body, the sweet attitude, and now…the ideal guy.

My guy. At least in my imagination.

I could feel myself deflate like a balloon, even as Caleb wrapped his arm around her shoulders and pulled her close, his hand resting on her hip as if they'd done this a thousand times before. And maybe they had.

"Hey, babe. You know Zoey, right?"

Amber's eyes brightened. "Mrs. Tanner's chemistry class, right? You sat near the front, I think."

I swallowed hard, my fingers playing with the edge of my shorts. "That's me. Hi, Amber."

"It's great to see you, Zoey. We're headed to our spot on the shore to watch the show. Want to join us?"

I really wanted to hate her. Really wanted to hate myself for continually having this crush on a guy who had a different girl every time I saw him. In every place I saw him, even if we weren't anywhere near school. I couldn't do any of that. So, instead, I shook my head, only looking at Amber and keeping my gaze off Caleb. I didn't want him to see. I never wanted him to see.

"I have to get back to my parents, but I just wanted to say hi." Another pause. "So, hi."

Though I didn't see pity on Amber's face—she *knew*. She knew about my crush. It had to be written all over my face. Only she didn't lay her claim on Caleb. Didn't act as if she were catty and mean and wanted me away. She just held him like she always could. And, maybe, for however long she had Caleb, she *could*.

She didn't make me feel small. Unseen.

That was all on me.

And Caleb Carr.

Because even at eight and fifteen, I couldn't get out of the way of my crush. And every time I saw him, he was with another girl.

I really needed to get over my feelings for Caleb.

No matter what my gooey heart said.

ZOEY & Caleb – Age 19

My fake ID had worked, and as my head swam and my friends giggled into their drinks, I knew I wasn't going to use it ever again.

Ever. Again.

My fingers were numb, and my ankles hurt from my high heels.

I didn't like being drunk, and I didn't know why I'd let myself get this way at all. It was Kyla's birthday, and we were celebrating. Only now, Kyla and Kayti were off with two guys they'd met, and I was standing by the bar, my shoes too tight, and the third guy of that trio with his hands on my butt.

"I should go home," I tried to say, only it sounded

garbled like I couldn't speak as I should. How many shots had the guys bought us? Damn it. This was stupid. I *knew* this was stupid, but my head hurt, and I just wanted to go to bed.

"I'll get you home, baby," the guy whispered, his breath on my neck. Bile slid up my throat, and I pushed the guy off. Matt? Yes, Matt was his name.

"I'm okay. I'm going to get a cab." I got my purse and tried to walk to my friends, who were currently in the booth making out with their guys.

"They're busy, baby. I'll get you home."

I ignored him. "Kyla?"

"Hey, girl," Kyla said, giggling. "Happy birthday to me! Are you going home with Matt?" She wasn't whispering, though everyone in the bar was dancing and drunk, so no one cared what she said.

"No, I'm going home. Are you okay?"

She nodded. "We're fine. You should go home with Matt."

I held back a shudder. I didn't like being drunk, and I wasn't sure I liked drunk Kyla either. Maybe it was just the booze in my system.

"I'm going home."

"Okay, doll. See you Monday!" Then she went back to kissing Chad, and I shook my head, turning on my too-high heels to head out to get a cab. Matt's hands were on my hips as soon as I turned, and I pulled away.

"Thanks for the drinks, but I need to go home."

"I'll get you outside, baby," he said. I never hated being called *baby* before. And yet, with him, I really didn't want to hear it again. Every time he said the word, it sounded sickly sweet and made me want to take a shower.

I just needed to get away from him and this night.

"I'm okay. Thanks, though." I made my way through the bar, trying to stay on my heels as people bumped into me. Tonight was so stupid. I shouldn't have used my fake ID. I shouldn't have had a drink—or four.

It was going to be okay. I would get home.

I made my way to the curb where the cabs usually came since this was the strip of my college town where all the bars were, when Matt grabbed my hips again.

"Let me get you home, baby. We can finish our night."

I pushed at him, fear gnawing at my belly. I had my phone in my hand, only I wasn't thinking clearly, and couldn't move out of his grasp.

"No. I want to go home. Alone."

"Baby."

"She said no," a deep voice said from our side, and Matt's grip tightened painfully on my hips.

"Get the fuck out of here, bro. No one asked you."

I raised my knee hard, and Matt grunted, pushing me back so I stumbled into the thick pole behind me.

"Bitch."

"Get your hands off her."

I tripped over my heels, and then soft hands were on me. I flinched and looked into green eyes that were unfamiliar but kind.

"Sorry, sorry. Are you okay? I'm Heather. Caleb is taking care of that guy. Are you all right? Should we call someone?"

I blinked, suddenly far too sober. I tore my gaze away from Heather and looked at the man I knew. The one who had always been part of my dreams.

Caleb.

Of course, it was Caleb Carr. Here. Miles from home. Still here when I needed him—and when I didn't want to see him. It only made sense. This was the way of things with us.

Caleb punched Matt in the face, and people started to gather around, talking to each other and shouting. It was too much, and I knew I was going to throw up. I shouldn't be here. Caleb shouldn't be here.

"I'm…I'm fine. I just want to go home."

Caleb turned at the sound of my voice, his eyes dark even under the streetlights. "Zoey-girl. You okay?"

"I'm fine. I…I'm getting a cab. Don't hurt him."

His brows rose as he looked down at Matt on the ground, who currently clutched his head and groaned.

"I just want to go home."

"We'll take you home," Caleb growled.

I shook my head and almost threw up from the dizziness the movement caused. "I'm fine."

"We're taking you home. Heather, get the cab."

"Sure thing, hon. We'll get your friend home." She squeezed my arms in affection, even as Caleb stepped over Matt's prone body, and the crowd began to disburse.

"I just want to go home," I whispered, not sure anyone could hear me.

Caleb's gaze never left mine as he slipped off his leather jacket and wrapped it around my shoulders. "We'll get you there, Zoey-girl. Trust me. I've got you."

Tears slid down my cheeks, and my body started to shake as I dug my fingers into the warm leather. Caleb didn't hold me. Didn't tell me everything would be okay.

No one touched me.

No one talked.

Because there was nothing to say. My so-called friends hadn't been there. The boy—no, the *man*—from my past had been there.

Again.

ZOEY & Caleb – Age 25

I hated the cold. Okay, sure, I lived in Colorado and was used to it, but it had nothing on the cold of Alaska.

Why Amy had to get married to her soulmate in the so-called Alaskan wilderness for a full-on glamping wedding at a log cabin suite in the woods was beyond me. However, she was my friend and had invited me to the wedding. So, here I was, cold, in a dress I hated, and ready to take off my shoes.

I'd met Amy while working at a flower shop in Denver. I would miss her when she made her final move up to Alaska. She'd met a bush pilot who had come to Denver for work and had fallen in love quickly. Now, she was uprooting her life and moving to the wilderness. I loved Amy and wished her the best. But I missed home.

I'd moved around enough for college and my first real job. Now, I was back in Denver and about to open my own shop if things went well over the next few months. I wanted to settle. I wanted to find love and heart and start my life.

I just wanted to be happy.

As if I'd conjured him from thin air, a voice from my past echoed behind me, and I turned to see the one person I always wanted to see yet never wanted to.

"Caleb," I whispered, then cleared my throat. "Why on earth are you in Alaska?" I blurted.

Caleb flashed that grin that always did things to my insides. "Zoey-girl. I should ask you the same damn thing." He opened his arms, and I went into them quickly. It was almost as if we always did this. As if it hadn't been years since we'd seen each other.

We never talked about that night at the bar. Never needed to. I was fine, and he'd been there. My knight in shining armor. One who wasn't mine at all.

He smelled of soap and that candle I loved so much that everyone said scented of *man*. He reminded me of home. And at that thought, I pulled away quickly and ran my hands down my brown velvet dress.

"Seriously. I didn't know you knew Amy."

"I don't. I'm friends with Don. He's flown me a few places for work." At my blank look, he continued. "I'm a boilermaker. Sometimes, I work on the oil line. Depends on the season."

"I have no idea what that is," I said, laughing.

"Not many people do."

"Caleb?" A woman with a red dress and even redder lips came up to his side and slid her hand around his waist. "You left me all alone." She patted his chest with her perfectly manicured fingers, and I curled my hands so she couldn't see the nicks and scrapes that came with my work. My hands would never be pretty, and I was fine with that. Though seeing Caleb's date in all her perfect glory just made me want to hide.

I hated that.

"Sorry, babe, just saw a friend I hadn't seen in a

while. Charlene, this is Zoey. We went to school together."

"What a small world," Charlene purred, giving me a little wave before putting her hands back on Caleb. I didn't blame her one bit. "Nice to meet you."

"Nice to meet you, too," I said quickly. "I should get going. Wedding party duties."

"Good to see you, Zoey-girl."

Charlene's grasp tightened, and I stepped back. "You, too. Sometime, we'll have to meet in Denver again, and not other places around the world."

"Sometime," he repeated, and then I was off, needing my space, needing to breathe. Seeing Caleb again was like a hit to the chest, and I couldn't focus.

I didn't know if I still had my crush. I didn't think about him daily anymore, but as soon as I saw him, it had tried to come back full-force.

I reminded myself that he was once again with a date. Once again with a woman who wasn't me.

And I was just fine with that.

I had to be.

Because Caleb wasn't mine.

He never would be.

ZOEY & Caleb − Age 28

Home. This was my home. I finally owned my florist

shop in truth. I was my own boss and only answered to the bank. This was *mine*.

I got to play and work with flowers every day. This would be my future. I couldn't wait to get my hands dirty —and probably bloody, thorns were the worst!—again.

I needed to go home and get to bed, but I didn't think I would be able to sleep. I already had orders waiting and would meet with a couple of wedding planners tomorrow. For tonight, though, it was all mine.

A tap on the glass pulled a scream from my throat. I turned to the window at the front of my shop, my hand on my phone, the other on my heart.

"Caleb?" I gasped, and he gave me that damn grin of his. I really hated it, even while I loved it.

"*Open up*," he mouthed, and I quickly went to the door.

"What are you doing here? I thought you were still in Alaska."

He shook his head. I couldn't read his eyes in the dark to tell what he was thinking. "I'm back."

Back.

I swallowed hard, trying to get my bearings. I hated that he did this to me. After two decades of it, you'd think I should be used to it by now.

"Amelia didn't tell me. Welcome back."

He shrugged. "She doesn't know."

My eyes widened.

"Don't worry, Zoey-girl. She'll know tomorrow. Wanted to surprise her and the others. Saw you working here and figured I'd check out your new place."

I blinked, trying to catch up. "Oh, well, I was just heading home, and it's dark. Maybe tomorrow?" When I could breathe.

"I can do that." He put his hands in his pockets and rocked back on his heels. "Need me to walk you to your car?"

I saw it then, the worry in his gaze. "I'm fine. Have been since that night. Thank you. Again." There. I'd mentioned it. Now, I didn't need to bring it up again. I didn't have nightmares or anything. I was safe. But I was still embarrassed.

"Don't thank me, Zoey-girl. And good."

"Caleb?"

Of course. At this point, it was inevitable. A woman with beautiful brown skin and killer hair walked towards us. She grinned at the two of us and slid her hand into his.

I mean, why not, right?

"Renita, this is Zoey, the girl I told you about."

He'd talked about me? No, I wasn't going there.

"Oh, hi!" Renita leaned forward and kissed my cheek, surprising me. "My sister is getting married soon, and she's looking for a florist. Hence Caleb mentioning you." She went on and on about the wedding, and I tried to tune in, but I was tired, and every time I was near Caleb, my brain did horrible things. Like not pay attention. "Anyway, I used to work with Caleb up in Alaska. Now, he's working down here in Denver again. It's fate, right?"

I didn't look over at Caleb, I couldn't. I kept my gaze on Renita, and she grinned, the most beautiful soul shining through her eyes.

"Fate, that sounds about right," I said, knowing it was the truth.

Because Caleb being home was fate. It had to be.

It just couldn't be mine.

ZOEY & Caleb – Age 30

I'd watched Caleb Carr fall into lust countless times throughout my life. In every corner of the world, fate brought him across my path. And yet it wasn't the right time.

Now, it had to be.

Because I wasn't going to watch any longer. I was going to be a part of it. I was ready for Caleb Carr to fall in love.

With me.

Chapter 2

Caleb

I SLID MY HAND ACROSS THE SMALL TABLE AND SQUEEZED Robin's fingers, grinning at her.

"You are a very wicked man, Caleb," Robin purred before taking her hand back. She picked up her glass of merlot and took a sip.

I leaned back in my chair and shook my head. "There's nothing wicked about me, Robin. Never has been." Okay, that was probably a lie, but that was fine with me. I liked Robin. She was sweet, had a brilliant head on her shoulders, and a killer body.

Her long, black hair flowed down her back, and she had recently cut her bangs so they lay thick across her eyebrow line. I had only really noticed because she'd mentioned it to me when I saw her last at the bar that I went to regularly.

Not that I indulged all the time, but after a long day, especially when life went to hell like it seemed to be doing a lot these days, I needed a drink. Or at least needed to be near the noise of other people.

Then I would go home and laugh at my solitude, something I was getting much better at in my old age.

"Now you're not paying attention to me," Robin said, tapping her fingernail on her glass. I didn't understand how she kept such great nails, considering that she typed for most of the day. She was a computer programmer—one of the best, according to her and anyone in the field who had ever spoken about her.

I was decent with computers, but nowhere near her level. So, if I ever needed to hack something or troubleshoot an issue with my laptop, she was the person to call. She'd charge an arm and a leg, but she was apparently worth that and more.

"Sorry. Woolgathering."

"That's fine. Are you going to tell me what you're thinking about?"

"That brain of yours," I said honestly.

Her eyes brightened. "That's better than talking about any other part of my anatomy, as most guys tend to do."

I snorted and took a sip of my vodka and water. I

wasn't going to finish it, but it was good for appearances. I was mostly on the water these days.

"You have other assets, as well," I said, grinning. "Ones I'm open to talking about if you're in the mood." A total line, but it was rote at this point. When had I become jaded?

"Yes, and I tend to like those assets." Her gaze traveled down to her very impressive cleavage, and then she laughed, making her boobs jiggle just enough. Dear God, I was going to lose my mind. But she knew that, and she was good at exploiting it. I liked a woman who was confident with her mind and body and knew exactly who she was.

I used to be that same type of person. Confident, happy, and knew what I was doing. These days? Not so much. But I didn't want to get into that. I didn't want to get serious or think about anything but what we were up to for the night.

Because this wasn't going to be serious. Nothing I ever did was serious. And every date that I had knew that going in. Not that I was an asshole or scared of commitment or anything, but I had plans. And before I moved back to Denver, those plans hadn't included women other than for the short-term. For the long-term? Not so much.

Dating when I was in Alaska had been interesting,

and I hadn't done it all that often considering the ratio of men to women where I had been living.

Dating in Denver? Well, I was at the age where everyone wanted to settle down, and I didn't know what I wanted yet. Not with everything that had happened recently. But, no, I wasn't going to think about that. Not now, at least.

"Anyway, how are you liking your new job outside of the wilderness?" Robin asked as the waiter set down our meals. I had ordered the fish, and she got the steak. My mouth salivated for the filet, but I was being good. Less red meat, and less alcohol, even though I was sipping a little vodka tonight.

"Denver is its own wilderness, even though it's a little different from Alaska."

"It's so funny that most people think that Denver, like Texas, must be filled with cowboys and is the Wild Wild West. And then, us Denverites, or Denveronians, what-ever they call us, all think that Alaska must be much of the same."

"What do they call people from Denver?

"Happy?" Robin asked and then laughed.

"That fish looks amazing."

I shrugged and looked down at my plate. "Want a bite?"

"I would love some. Would you like some steak?"

"I should say no, but I'd love a bite."

"Watching your red meat intake?"

"Hey, I'm thirty. I should."

"I thought that's what they said at forty?"

"Apparently, thirty is the new forty and all that."

"I thought it worked the opposite way," she said with a laugh. We traded some of our meals. I moaned when I took a bite of the steak.

I missed red meat. My doctor said I needed to be careful, hence why I had moved from Alaska to Denver in the first place. And why I was no longer working out on the line at the new construction job, but rather running it from behind the scenes, and mostly on my tablet from behind a desk.

I was damn good at my job, but sometimes I missed working with my hands like I used to.

However, it was hard to do that when I wasn't sure what was coming.

"Well…I, for one, am glad that you're back in Denver," Robin said, grinning. "I think we went on a date what, ten years ago or so? When we were babies."

I snorted. "We *were* babies. We're completely different people now."

"That's good. Either that or you've gone through all of the women on the western hemisphere and now you have to circle back. Which isn't so good."

I almost choked on my water and shook my head. "I'm not that bad."

"You are. Except you never string anyone along. You're exactly who you say you are."

I frowned. "And what am I, exactly?"

Robin shook her head. "Nothing bad. Please don't take it badly. I'm ruining this. All I meant is that anyone going on a date with you knows it's not going to be serious. And no one goes in trying to change you. If they do, then they're in for a rude awakening."

I looked down at my fish and played with the fork in my hand. "I didn't realize I was that predictable."

"Oh, shush. I'm just as predictable. I haven't had a serious relationship in the ten years since we've seen each other. In fact, I've been so focused on work, it was a surprise that I was even at that bar when I saw you again. And now, coming out to dinner with you... We're doing this lovely surf and turf thing, and we're not going to ruin it by talking about serious things. Only happy stuff."

I nodded and forced a smile. "Okay, I can do that."

I grinned and let the disappointment seep from me. It wasn't like I really wanted a serious relationship with Robin. I just didn't like the fact that, apparently, it was tattooed on my forehead that I wasn't the person one went to for a serious relationship. Maybe it was asking too much for me not to feel like a complete asshole. Or perhaps that was just who I was.

"Okay, other than going to that bar and working—

and apparently trying not to walk out on me because I'm acting like an idiot—what do you do for fun these days, Caleb?"

I shook my head, pulling myself back to the conversation. "You're not an idiot. Sorry. Apparently, I'm just grumpy."

"Women love grumpy men, Caleb. You should know that."

I gave her my best smirk. "Oh, that I do, darling."

Her laughed trilled, and I just shook my head, joining her in the laughter.

"You really need to use that smirk on everyone. It does wonders."

"Glad I could help."

We talked about nothing, and that was fine. I wasn't going home with her tonight, I hadn't planned on it going in. It was simply nice being with another human when I didn't have to sit at home and wonder about mortality and everything that came with life—or the lack thereof.

After we'd finished our meals, we paid the bill and went to the valet for our cars. We had met at the restaurant rather than me picking her up, and from the look on her face, I knew that she knew we weren't going home together. I wasn't in the mood, and it was clear that she'd figured that out on her own.

"This was nice, Caleb. Maybe we should do it again in ten years."

"You really think you're going to be single in ten years?" It was an honest question. Robin was a fantastic, talented, brilliant, and beautiful woman. She deserved happiness however it came.

"Maybe. I have work to do. Men get in the way."

"You know, that's kind of what we do. It's our legacy."

"You're a good man, Caleb. I hope that you're not single in ten years, even if part of me kind of wishes you would be."

I only hoped I'd *be* here in ten years. I quickly pushed that thought from my mind because I wasn't going to think about it.

"It was good seeing you, Robin." I kissed her on her cheek as the valet pulled up. As she slid into her car, my gaze met someone else's, not Robin's. Someone from my past—and my present. And maybe my future, only not in the way that I might want it.

Zoey stood on the other side of the street, her hands full of bags from wherever she had been shopping. I knew she worked hard, and sometimes she didn't get to the grocery store until late in the evening. My brother had mentioned it to me once because his woman was best friends with Zoey.

Zoey had been in and out of my life for as long as I

could remember. She had always been there, literally in every hemisphere I'd ever visited. Oddly, she was always there.

She gave me a halfhearted smile from across the way, looked at Robin in her car, and then laughter filled her eyes. I didn't know what that meant. Then again, I never could read Zoey. She was so good at hiding who she was, that I sometimes forgot to search deeper. And every time I thought I should, she pulled away, and then I didn't see her again for a while. Now, it was kind of hard to hide when I saw her practically every day. Or at least every week. Sometimes, it felt like every day because I spent more time with my family now than I ever had in the past, or at least the past decade.

Zoey shook her head and walked off to where she was presumably parked. I almost wanted to walk out and make sure she got to her car okay. An image of that asshole back at the bar when we were younger filled my mind. It had been what? Eleven years ago, now?

It still filled me with rage when I thought about it. I hadn't been able to kill that asshole. Hadn't been able to do anything except pull him off of her and get her home. I didn't even remember the girl I was with at the time. Not that I remembered every woman I had ever been with, but I tried not to forget them. We hadn't done anything more than hold hands and kiss that night. She had been shaken by what had happened with Zoey, too, and I was so pissed off that I hadn't wanted to do anything but get her home just like I had gotten Zoey home.

Thinking about it now, I didn't remember her name. I remembered Zoey's face. And I was never going to get that image out of my mind. Holy hell, how was I supposed to do that when all I could do was imagine her drunk again? The asshole forcing the issue. Luckily, I had been there. Jesus Christ.

What if I hadn't been there?

What if she had been forced to go home with him?

My hands fisted, and I made myself not think about that.

"Sir? Your car is here."

I gave the valet a nod and a tip, then slid into the driver's seat. I didn't want to go home. Didn't want to be alone. I hated the sound of my empty house. I hadn't even put anything up on the walls yet, and I'd been living there for long enough that I should have. My little sister Amelia constantly annoyed me about it. One day, I was going to come home, and there would be pictures and art on my walls thanks to her and my sister-in-law, as well as my future sister-in-law. The women would take care of it, if I let them.

It was just hard to want to put permanence on a place where I hadn't really had permanence until now.

Honestly, I didn't know if I was ever going to find anything permanent again. Not when I was still waiting.

Still fucking waiting.

I put the car in drive and headed towards Devin's.

I could have gone to Dimitri's, only he was at least an hour south. Since it was still pretty early considering that I'd had an early dinner with Robin, driving down to surprise my brother and his very pregnant wife probably wouldn't be the smart thing, especially not with the likely traffic.

I didn't want to visit my little sister because Tucker was practically living there now, and imagining Amelia doing things I didn't want to think about wasn't high on my fun-things-to-do list. So, I would see Devin. Any of my siblings would open their homes to me in an instant. Even if I annoyed the fuck out of them, they would let me in. Like I would do for them.

I just didn't want to be alone.

When I pulled into the driveway, I was grateful to see the lights on, and shadows in the window. They didn't seem to be doing anything inappropriate, thank God, so I headed up to the door and knocked.

Erin answered, her hair piled on the top of her head, and a green face mask on her face.

"Hey there. Looking beautiful. Is green the new color?"

Her eyes widened, and she tapped her cheek and cursed.

"Crap. Devin!" She turned, and I followed her into the living room, closing and locking the door behind me.

"What is it, babe?" Devin asked from the kitchen.

"You let me answer the door with my face mask on."

Devin's head popped out of the kitchen door, and I grinned.

"Considering I'm wearing the same damn face mask as you right now, I figured you should be the one to answer."

"So, you knew I was going to?"

"Of course, I did, babe. You look beautiful."

I laughed. "And so do you, big brother. Love the new look."

"Fuck you. My pores are going to be amazing after this."

Erin beamed at us. "That is true. And next time, there's this pumpkin spice one that I love."

Devin raised his green brows. "That's just going to make me hungry."

"Great, now I want dessert," I grumbled.

"I thought you were on a date tonight?" Devin asked, bringing out some cheese and fruit.

Yum, cheese and fruit. Ever since our older brother Dimitri had married Thea, cheese had become a huge part of our lives. However, Thea was now very pregnant and couldn't have soft cheeses anymore. We'd all thought about maybe giving it up with her, but we couldn't. Not when soft cheese existed in the world.

"I was on a date."

"That bad?" Erin asked, taking a piece of cheese from the board before Devin could set it down.

"No, it was nice. I just wasn't in the mood for it to go any further."

"That sounds reasonable. Are you going to eat all of our cheese?" she asked as I nibbled another piece.

"What? It's really good," I answered with a mouth full of cheese.

"I have more in the fridge that I can cut up. Or I can make my lazy brother do it for me." Devin kissed Erin on the lips before taking a seat next to her, cheese in hand. "Anything you wanted to talk about, or are you just here because you want to be?"

"No, I was bored and figured I'd see what you guys were up to. Dimitri's was too far, and last time I was at Amelia's, I walked in on something I never want to think about again."

Devin shuddered, and Erin giggled.

"She told me about that. There are some things siblings never need to see."

"Or talk about," I growled out.

"Or talk about," Erin agreed. "So, you're just here because you want to be?"

I shrugged. "I was gone awhile when I was in Alaska. Figured I'd say hi."

"We were just going to sit and watch a movie tonight. We're doing face masks and eating cheese. And, eventually, Erin wants to convince me to do a pedicure."

I snorted. "Can't you just go somewhere and get one? Seems easier than having to deal with feet."

Erin nodded and munched on her cheese. "Sure. Except, sometimes, you can do those little bags that you wrap around your feet, and then you have baby feet for a few months."

"Why would you want baby feet?" I asked.

"Because they're soft and pretty. Wait. Have you ever had a pedicure?"

I shrugged, and Devin snorted. "Really, bro?"

"You're wearing a face mask, don't even."

"Touché." A pause. "Was it good?"

"Considering that my feet are in work boots for most of the time when I'm awake, it felt fucking amazing. I didn't let them do any polish or anything because I don't really need color on my toes. If that's your thing, then go for it. However, I liked the little cheese grater thing they used."

"Please don't talk about the cheese grater thing for your feet while we're eating cheese," Erin snapped.

I looked at her, shaking my head. "Good point. However, I'm not joining you for a pedicure."

"Then you have to join in on the face masks if you're going to eat our cheese." Erin jumped to her feet.

I shrugged. Might as well live for the moment while I could still live at all. Not that I said those words aloud. I didn't even want to *think* those words.

"Okay, I'll bite. Can I have the pumpkin spice one?"

"We're saving that for next time. You get green like both of us."

"Anything you want."

She rushed off to where I assumed the face masks were, and Devin stared at me. "Anything on your mind?"

I shook my head, my gaze down on my phone even though there wasn't anything on the screen. Devin would be able to tell something was up. Just like Amelia would. Like Dimitri. And I was worried. Worried because I didn't have any answers.

So, I wasn't going to think about anything. I was simply going to breathe, eat some cheese, clean my pores, and be near my family.

Because I didn't have any answers. And, sometimes, living was the only way to just be.

Chapter 3

Zoey

"I'M GETTING MARRIED!"

I just grinned, shaking my head as I sat down on the familiar couch in my parents' home. My sister danced in the middle of the living room, careful not to bump into the coffee table. My mother beamed at her. My little sister was getting *married*. *Finally*, in her estimation.

My mother had probably wished…no, there was no probably about it, my mother *had* wished that I would be the first one to get married. Or at least engaged. Or maybe be in a serious relationship. After all, I was the older sister. That was how things were supposed to go. Only that's not how life worked. I *did* have a plan, however. At least, an endgame. I needed to come up with the rest of the scheme.

"I'm so happy, I can't even stand it," Mom said before she stood up and took Lacey's hands into her own. The two looked at each other, their eyes bright and a little teary before they bent slightly, resting their foreheads together. "My little baby's getting married. You're going to be such a beautiful bride, Lacey. Such a beautiful bride."

I swallowed hard and stood up, walking around the coffee table so I could join in. It wasn't that they forgot I was there, it was more like it had always been the two of them against the world. And, honestly, I'd never been the least bit jealous about that. How could I be when Lacey had been through so much?

My mother and Lacey had spent countless hours together in the emergency room, in the hospital, in the bathroom with Lacey puking her guts out, and my mother had practically slept in Lacey's room, cuddling her baby daughter when my sister was going through treatments.

The two had bonded in a way that I would never be able to do with either of them. And I would never begrudge them for that. Because I didn't know what it felt like to look at my own mortality, especially at that young an age, and wonder if I was going to wake up the next day. I didn't know what it was like to think that I could possibly outlive my daughter.

So, no, I never envied the fact that the two of them had their special bond. One I didn't share with even my father. Even though I still sometimes liked to consider myself a Daddy's girl, I didn't have that special bond with him either—and neither of us felt the lack. However, I did want to be part of Lacey and Mom's moment, if only for a bit. Because, after all, my little sister, the one I had been so afraid I would lose multiple times in my life, was getting married.

"You are going to be an amazing bride," I said, coming up to put my hands on each of their backs. They looked at me then, their eyes wide, tears trickling down their cheeks.

"I can't wait. John is such an amazing man. And he's all mine."

I smiled, shaking my head. John Yi *was* a wonderful man—one I didn't really know all that well because he was a cardiologist and worked long hours. He rarely came to the same family dinners I attended. My mother knew him, and my dad really liked him. And because of all of that, I was *all there* for this wedding. And I knew from the bit that I had gotten to know him, that he loved my baby sister with every ounce of his soul. What more could I ask for in a future brother-in-law?

"He's going to make you very happy, just as I know you're going to make yourself very happy," I added.

Lacey rolled her eyes and pulled away so she could do a little butt wiggle again before turning towards me. "Oh, stop it. I'm not like you. I want to get married and have babies and have a wonderful life." Lacey swallowed hard, and I wanted to reach out and hug her. Only I didn't, because she wouldn't want that. "And I know that having babies naturally is probably not in the cards for me, but I'm fine," she added.

My mother opened her mouth to speak when Lacey quickly shook her head. "No. I've already gone through that mourning stage in my life. John and I are already looking into adoption, and possibly talking about surrogacy." She glanced at me hopefully, and I held up my hands.

"Whoa there, let's do the wedding first. And then maybe we can talk about my uterus."

She just rolled her eyes at me, and I held back a shudder. I would do many things for my sister, and if she and John asked, I might actually do that. Only that was a long way off, and I needed to get through the idea of it first. And then there was the whole pregnancy thing... I really did not want to go through pregnancy. Not that it wasn't beautiful and wonderful for many women. I just never really thought that was my thing. It changed your body, it changed your life, and it was a huge hormonal and emotional burden. And with surrogacy, you didn't get the baby in the end. She hadn't even asked yet, and I was overthinking things for no reason. After all, John had three sisters, three wonderful siblings, two of whom already had children of their own. We knew their uteruses worked just fine.

I really needed to stop digging myself into a mental hole.

"Okay, so, where do we start?" I asked, and both my mother and my sister looked at each other before they burst out laughing.

"Oh, honey, we've already started." Mother reached down and picked up the very large binder with the tablet resting on top.

"I thought that was like a baby book," I said, frowning.

"No, no, no, this is The Wedding Book." She said the words as if they were all capitalized, and there should be angels singing.

I frowned.

"The wedding book? Wait, didn't you have one like that when you were younger and used to play with it while you were in the hospital bed?"

My mother winced while Lacey nodded. Mom didn't like to talk about that time. Mostly because, every time she did, everyone got super sad and started thinking about cancer again. Lacey didn't have a problem with saying the C-word, and neither did I. Mom was another story, so we were both careful around her.

"It's not the exact same wedding book because, you know, I'm not six anymore. Though it is where it all began." We laughed. "We really have been planning this wedding for my entire life." Lacey shrugged. "I didn't know if I'd ever have a wedding. Or if I'd have a prom or learn to drive or do any of that. So, I wanted to live with the idea that I *could*. With sparkly dresses and flowers galore. I wanted twinkle lights and a band, and I wanted my dad to dance with me and give me away. I wanted all of that. So, Mom and I made The Wedding Book. It's not going to be the same incarnation by the time we're done. However, I love the fact that I actually get to do this." She took a shaky breath. "It's not just a dream anymore."

I discreetly wiped at a tear as my mother blew her nose into a tissue. It had been over ten years since the last scare, and every day felt like borrowed time, even if Lacey was completely healthy. The damage that chemo and radiation and countless medical tests did to one's body changed everything. I was going to do anything my little sister asked, even if I had a feeling from the way that my mother and Lacey kept looking at each other, the word *Bridezilla* might be uttered. More than once.

"Okay. So, apparently, the question of where do *we*

start has already been answered. How about where do *I* start?"

Lacey bounced on her toes and came over to me, her arms outstretched. I hugged her tightly, kissing the top of her head. She was only a couple of inches shorter than I was. However, I was wearing heels, while Lacey was barefoot like a little pixie.

"Well, first, I need to ask the big question."

I took a step back, my eyebrows raised. "You do? I thought John already popped the question."

"Haha. Will you be my maid of honor?"

Warmth spread through me, and I grinned. "Really? I thought you were going to ask Mary Kate."

Mary Kate and Lacey had been best friends for what seemed like forever. They had met in the children's oncology ward, Lacey being there for herself, while Mary Kate had been there for her sister. Mary Kate's sister hadn't made it, something that hurt to even think about. Through their shared pain and similar ages, Lacey had formed such a deep and everlasting friendship with Mary Kate that I thought they would be shoe-ins for each other's maids of honor.

"I thought about it. In the end, I decided I want you. You're my big sister. I've known you longer. And you're one of my best friends, too."

This time, I wiped away my tears and kissed Lacey on the cheek. "Of course, I'll say yes."

"Good. Because I have such a long list for you."

I groaned. "You're really only making me your maid of honor because I can actually adhere to lists rather than Mary Kate, who kind of likes to go with the flow."

"Well, that might be part of it…though not the only part."

I had been bamboozled. Completely and utterly hoodwinked. I loved my little sister, though, so I'd make it work. Like always. I would deal with it. Even though I had a feeling this was not going to be fun at all.

"Now, I have your binder here, too." She picked up the other notebook that I hadn't noticed before. "This is just the starter pack."

The thing weighed like ten pounds.

"Starter pack?"

"Yes. This isn't all of it. And a lot of what we'll be doing will be digital. That way, we can all upload it to the cloud and be up-to-date at any given moment if any emergencies arise, or if we need to have last-minute meetings."

"Meetings?" I knew there was a little bit of panic in my voice, but I couldn't help it. Dear God. I had a full-time job. I owned my own business. I had best friends of my own and a life. Not a huge one, and not one with dating. Although I had already promised myself that I was going to work on the latter. This whole wedding thing might actually get in the way of that.

Dear God. I started to look through the notebook, swallowing hard. Everything was neatly organized and labeled, with ideas for flowers, music, the dancing, linens, dishware, where they would register… Everything was color-coded and in order of precedence. There was a whole section for the dress, as well as addresses of the attendants. The colors hadn't been picked yet. However, there were five different areas where Lacey could choose. And from there, apparently, I would be able to triangulate exactly what would happen. There was a damn flow chart in the thing.

No wonder she wanted this to be digital.

My sister was a machine and seriously needed to be a wedding planner instead of working as an administrative assistant.

"Lacey, you only got engaged like a month ago."

"I know. And I'm already behind. It's still okay, though, because I have a plan. With the move coming up, we had to push the wedding up a little earlier than I wanted it. Even with that, we're going to make this work. I already have all the starter appointments ready, and we're going to make this happen. John might not be here for all of it, though. Because, you know, he has work."

I did, and his work was the reason that Lacey was moving. My baby sister was relocating across the country because John was getting an amazing fellowship at another hospital. One that he had been trying to get for a few years, and now there was an opening. He was going to be in a position to become one of the top cardiologists in the country, and my baby sister was going to go with him and most likely start having that family and being the best doctor's wife ever in the history of marriage. At least, that's what I figured her to-do list would have on it.

Checklist one: get married.

Checklist two: have a family.

Checklist three: take over the world.

"Is John going to be a part of any of this?"

Lacey beamed. "Of course, he is. He's going to help me pick out everything. With work, though, he might not actually be there for each meeting and planning strategy. That's why I've made this detailed system, so he only has to choose from what we've narrowed down. After that, then it's all the meetings, and I want you to be there every step of the way."

"So, you're not hiring a wedding planner?" I said, blinking.

"No, I've got this. So does Mom."

Mom reached out and gripped Lacey's hand. "We've got this, honey." She turned to me. "And, of course, you'll help with the flowers, won't you?"

Help. With the flowers. Oh, no. Did they want me to do this for free? The size and scale of this wedding, at least from what I could tell, meant that it was going to take a lot of time, energy, manpower, and money to get done.

There must've been something showing on my face because my mother pinched her lips as if she had sucked on a lemon, and my sister rolled her eyes.

"We're going to pay you, of course."

"I didn't say anything."

"You didn't have to. I know your job is really hard," she said and then winced. "Okay, so that sounded like I was placating you. I *know* it's an actual job. I don't want the flowers for free. I want the best of the best. And you're the best."

"Well, that was a nice thing to say."

"I can be nice during all this. I might be a little anal-retentive. I want everything perfect for the best day of my life. But I'm going to be nice about it. Promise."

Her voice got a little shriller as she said that, and the word *Bridezilla* once again slipped through my mind.

My baby sister was the sweetest, most wonderful, kindest girl I knew. Yes, sometimes she got in her own way a bit and focused on what she wanted, mostly because that's what had happened throughout her childhood when we were dealing with everything having to do with cancer. She was still amazing. And wonderful to me.

I just had a feeling that those traits might be buried a little deeper under the Engaged Lacey marker.

Hopefully, once Married Lacey showed her face,

things would get back to normal. However, I had a feeling these next few months would be long ones.

"Anyway, you'll be my maid of honor, and Mary Kate will be right under you. And then John's sisters will be there."

"And they all agreed?"

"Yes. John and I asked them when we were at dinner the other night. I know I'm asking you last. I needed you to be here because I wanted to do it in person. I hope that's okay."

"It's really okay. I just want to make sure I do this right for you."

"You will." That sounded more like a threat than a promise. I rolled with it. My mother impatiently looked between us, her toe tapping.

"What's wrong, Mom?" I asked, keeping my voice light.

"We don't have a lot of time to waste. We need to get going."

"I need to head to work, though," I said. "I can only give you about thirty minutes right now."

My mother's lips pursed again, and I put a bright smile on my face. "I will do my best to show up whenever I can. You know I'm shorthanded right now during this season..." I shook my head. "I'll make it work. I promise."

"You will," my sister said, squeezing my hand a little

tighter than was warranted.

Time to get through the initial phases then, since I figured it was going to be a long couple of months. "Now, there's five of us as your attendants?"

"Yes, and John will have five groomsmen, as well. Actually, you know one of them. Caleb? He knows John from something or other. I don't really remember how they met. You know, Denver is the smallest big city ever." I kept a bright smile on my face, even as I blinked.

"Caleb Carr?"

"Yes, Amelia's big brother. He's so hot."

"Lacey," my mother warned, though her lips quirked.

"I'm engaged, Mother, not a nun."

My mother glared for a moment before she grinned. "Well, those Carr brothers sure do know how to fill out a suit."

I groaned, closed my eyes, and tried to count to ten. "That's an image I never want to think about again."

"What, the Carr brothers in suits?" Lacey asked, all too sweetly.

"No, my mother thinking about that." Lacey and I laughed, and my mom just rolled her eyes.

"I don't know why you think that you and your little sister just showed up one day thanks to a stork. I'll have you know...your father cuts a nice line in his suits, too. In fact, just the other day—"

"No, no, no. None of that." I cut her off, laughing. "I know you're only trying to get a rise out of me. Stop."

"Speaking of rises," my mother began, and Lacey burst out laughing.

I closed my eyes and counted to ten, trying to put all of those thoughts out of my mind. "What did I do to deserve this? Why is this happening?"

"Because you're a smartass. Just like your father. And I love him. So, I love you." My mother kissed me on the cheek and then went back to the tablet in her hand. "Okay, so there's five attendants on each side, and we're looking at what? Three hundred people?" My mother said, and Lacey nodded.

My eyes widened, my mind boggled. "Three hundred? I don't think I know three hundred people."

"You know three hundred people in your life. And I have made a lot of friends over my lifetime. And so has John. We want them to be there for our special day."

"That's going to be a lot of money, Lacey."

Lacey nodded. "I know. And I'm paying for some of it. Mom and Dad are paying for some of it. John's paying for some of it. And so are his parents. We've got this. I promise, we're not going over budget or crazy. There's a reason that I went into so much detail about everything in that notebook. I spent years playing with weddings just for fun because I loved the idea of planning them. I know what I want my budget to be. I don't need the best of everything. Yet, I still want to feel pretty. Like it's my day."

Shamed, I hugged my sister tightly again. "I'm sorry. I know you do. And it is your day, you should feel that way. You're so practical, even if your head's in the clouds more than mine at times."

"For a florist, sometimes you're the least romantic person I know."

"Maybe because the thorns always make me bleed," I said and then kissed Lacey's cheek. "Okay, ignore me and just tell me what to do."

"Because John doesn't have any brothers, and he wasn't sure how to pick between his friends, he flipped a coin for who was going to be his best man."

I nodded, a little wary. "O-o-o-kay."

"That means Caleb was actually chosen as his best man," she said with a wince.

"Why are you wincing?" my mother asked.

I knew. Because Lacey knew. Lacey knew about my crush. She had always known about it. The fact that she had been delicate about the idea of whether I knew Caleb had put me at ease. Because she knew. And I was going to have to work side by side with Caleb Carr.

He wasn't my nemesis. He wasn't my future.

Yet.

"Okay, does he know that he's the best man?"

"I don't know. But you guys are going to be working

very closely." Her brows rose. "Is that going to be okay with you?"

"Why wouldn't that be okay with her?" my mother asked. We both ignored her.

"It'll be fine. I promise. However, that does seem a little coincidental," I said.

Lacey held up her hands. "I swear, it really wasn't on purpose."

"Why would it matter if it was on purpose?" my mother asked, and once again, we ignored her.

"Oh, good." I paused. "Will Caleb have a lot of duties? I mean, I didn't think a best man had a long list or anything. Pretty much the ring, the stag party, and get John there."

"Well, this best man's going to do a lot because, like I said, John's going to be really busy…"

Lacey trailed off, and I froze.

"How much do you want me to work with Caleb?"

"As much as you need to," she said, and I had a feeling that maybe that coin hadn't been so improbably statistical after all.

My sister, the happiest girl in the world, the woman who might as well be a Bridezilla one day, was playing matchmaker.

Even as something warmed inside me, I really hoped this wasn't going to be a mistake.

Chapter 4

Caleb

"Wait. What?" I asked as I leaned forward across the café table. I pushed the coffee from beside my elbow so I wouldn't spill it and, thankfully, missed the danish when I knocked my elbow into the small plate.

We were in a place called Taboo, that wasn't all that taboo from the outside. Maybe the owner was taboo, but I didn't know. Instead, it had really fucking good coffee and pastries…and cinnamon rolls. With that really thick frosting and the way they made the edges just perfect. I was a fan of the edges, not the centers. Of course, my sister called that sacrilegious, but I didn't want to go there.

And now, I was thinking about cinnamon rolls, and my mouth was watering. I had to keep my mind on track and on exactly what my friend John Yi was saying.

"Caleb. It's fine. It's not that much work."

I blinked over at John and just shook my head. "I said I'd be one of your groomsmen. Not the best man. Not that I'm not the best," I said with a wink and a loud laugh. "But don't you have like a cousin or something to do that? One that's known you forever?"

John shrugged, then went back to tearing at his napkin. John had always done that, ever since I'd met him. The guy got nervous and proceeded to tear a napkin into tiny little pieces or scraped the label off a beer bottle. It didn't matter if everything was going a hundred percent perfect in our lives, or if there was no stress at all, John would always find something to be anxious about. And he would pick. He would tear. I hated seeing it, mostly because I knew that John hated having that outward tell, so I ignored it.

Instead, I let out a sigh. "Sorry about that," I whispered.

"No, it's okay, really. And I do have other friends. I just consider you all equal. So, I created a bracket of sorts and flipped a coin to figure out exactly who was going to be my best man. You beat Matt by a head versus a tail."

I just shook my head. Of course, that's what John had done. My brilliant friend, who was socially awkward yet a really great guy.

I thought of myself as slightly socially awkward sometimes, though not as much as John. It mostly stemmed from the fact that over the past ten years or so, I had been around the world, mainly in the Alaskan wilderness, and I didn't interact with that many people. John had been one of those people, though, and now he was getting married. I liked his fiancée, but I didn't know her all that well. I did, however, know her big sister, Zoey. And that meant I had a feeling I knew exactly who was going to be the maid of honor.

Great. I liked Zoey. Except for the fact that every time I was near her, my dick decided to do things it shouldn't. It always pressed against my zipper, wanting out. I'd saw a meme once where...

Not going there.

"I'm honored, John. But I've never been a best man before. Not even in either of Dmitri's weddings."

"Devin?" John asked, and I nodded.

It would have been easy for me to be the best man, too, considering Devin had already done it once, but I had offered to let Devin take the best man place again for Dmitri. "Dimitri finally found his perfect person, so we wanted to do it right. You know?"

"Well, Lacey is going to be my one and only. I'm not doing this again. So, I really want you to be my best man. You're a good guy, you like Lacey, and you like me."

"We all like you, John."

John shrugged. "Maybe. But, it's still hard to forget those times in elementary school when kids made fun of my last name or how I looked, or the fact that I used to talk to myself when I was doing math problems."

"That's how you get math problems done quickly. You talk it through. It's fine." And it was fine, I really didn't care that John was quirky. Hell, so was I. I couldn't fix the fact that little kids were taught by their parents to be racist assholes, but I could either hold John's coat when he beat the shit out of them now, or beat the shit out of them myself. After all, if I were going to be his best man, I figured I would have to take matters into my own hands if things got out of hand.

"I'll be your best man," I said quickly, noticing the way John's shoulders started to droop. I liked John, I liked Lacey, I could do this. Not that I knew what I was doing.

"Great. And I swear it's not going to be a lot of work."

"So, I just have to like plan your stag party, right?"

John blushed. "No strippers or anything, okay?"

I snorted. "We're really not stripper kind of guys." Which would probably surprise anyone who thought they knew me. They all thought I was the bad boy or whatever the hell other label that they wanted to put on me. Sure, I'd been wild as a teen, gotten into a few scrapes, and gotten caught by cops a couple of times and sent home with the flashing lights in the window to wake my parents up. But I wasn't that kid anymore. And I had a lot more things to worry about now rather than when I was going to see my next pair of boobs.

"I'm not taking you out to some fancy tea or something," I said, grumbling.

John snorted. "Not that either. Maybe we'll go see a game or something. I don't know. You decide. I already have a lot of other decisions to make." He started to rub his temples, and I snorted.

"Lacey having fun?"

"I love her. I love her with every ounce of my being. But the number of spreadsheets that go into planning a wedding? There are flow charts, Caleb. Actual flow charts."

I smiled then, imagining Lacey running around John with a binder full of wedding plans. That sounded about right. "Is Zoey her best woman? No, maid of honor, right?"

"I think you should call her the best woman. She'd probably like that."

"Probably."

"Yes, she is. And I'm glad that you know her pretty well. Because I think Lacey wants the two of you guys to work together often."

There wasn't a tone of matchmaking or sly innuendo in that, simply serious wedding planning. Which was good. Because I wanted nothing to do with matchmaking. Or relationships. Or anything.

"Yeah, she's a good girl."

"Actually, she's a woman, so I wouldn't call her a girl, or she might get snappy about that."

"That is true," I said, thinking of the way she usually growled when I was around. I said things like that, mostly because I liked to needle her. It was either that or remember the night I almost hadn't been there in time. But I wasn't going to think about that now.

"Anyway, other than the stag party, what else do I have to do?"

"I don't know yet." John winced. "Lacey will give me a list. Or Lacey will give Zoey a list to give to you. Either way, I have a feeling you will be working together closely in the future."

My brows shot up. "Zoey has a full-time job and owns her own business. And I work full-time, too. How much time are we actually talking about?"

John shook his head. "Not too much. I hope not. It really just depends on how things go. You know?"

"I have no idea how to help you with this. But I'll make sure that you get to your wedding on time, and I'll hold the rings and your speech or whatever else you need. I'll be there for you. Promise."

"Thanks. I'm glad to know that I'll have you in my corner."

"Of course, I am. It's not like you can have your three sisters up there as your best man."

"You know, I asked, and they got all affronted. They're going to be in the wedding party, though. So, they'll be part of it. However, they refused to stand by my side. It's not like they're my sisters or anything. Blood, you know. *Blood*."

I laughed. "I'm glad that you're going to be part of this. And the rest of the guys."

"We have time. Not that much because you know I'm moving and, therefore, we don't have as much time as Lacey would like to revisit matters. But she's going to be my wife. And that's all that matters."

"Yeah, that's all that matters."

"It's like a future, you know? A real one. With the love of my life. I can't wait."

I sipped my coffee and nodded, trying to smile. A future. That would be nice. To know exactly where you were going and what would happen. I just didn't know. And I hated that I didn't. I rubbed my temple, realized I was doing it, and let my hands fall. My head didn't hurt, and I should be grateful for that. My palms weren't sweaty, and I didn't have to throw up. I didn't see things that I shouldn't.

I just didn't know what was coming next.

It was fine. I could still have a future. This didn't have to be the end.

"Anyway, I need to head back into work. Are you off for the afternoon?"

I nodded. "Yeah, I'm doing four tens for the next quarter or so to see how I like it."

"I've always wanted to do that, but I end up working five tens as it is."

I grinned. "Oh, I know exactly how that is. Now, though, I get overtime."

"That you do. I just get pain in my back. And probably an ulcer."

I rolled my eyes and said goodbye as John headed back to work. I sat there and finished my coffee, wondering what exactly it meant to be a best man. And what it would mean to work with Zoey day in and day out. Zoey, the one person who had been a constant in my life other than my family. And the one who seemed to haunt my dreams, even though she really shouldn't. In the end, it wouldn't matter, though. Because I wasn't going to make a move, I wasn't going to do anything about it.

Because I didn't have that type of future.

And if my fate really fucked me over, I wasn't going to have a future at all.

━━

Zoey

"I LOVE WEDDINGS." Amelia sighed from my side, and I barely resisted the urge to roll my eyes.

I was a florist. I *loved* everything about that special day. However, seeing two of my best friends walking on clouds as they discussed their own nuptials was a bit much, even for me. Not that I begrudged them their happiness. In fact, I was just as excited as they were usually. However, it was when they went all Disney princesses and sighed dreamily into their clasped hands that I wanted to laugh.

"I know you love weddings," I said, shaking my head.

"Don't you shake your head at me. One day, you too will be engaged, and you will have bride fever. I didn't even realize I was going to *get* bride fever. I honestly don't know how I feel about it. I've become this monster, and I'm not even truly planning the wedding yet." She wiggled her fingers, her engagement ring sparkling in the light. "I can't believe two weddings are coming. Other than your sister's!"

Erin snorted and shook her head, too. "I do *not* have bride fever."

Amelia and I met gazes before we burst out laughing.

"What? I did not have bride fever for my first wedding, and I'm not going to have it this time either."

"First, you were like a zygote the first time you got married," Amelia started, and I just went back to working on the hand-tied bouquets at my workstation. I had a million things to do, and only a few short hours to get them done. I'd finish on time, but I also needed to focus.

"Nice," Erin said, her voice a little biting. But still full of love. We were friends, after all. It's what we did.

"Second, you are already like three notebooks into your wedding planning."

"Well, that might be true, but we're all newly engaged, so I'm having fun with it. We haven't actually started the real planning."

I closed my eyes and groaned. "Let's not talk about wedding plans until I'm done with Lacey's. And then we can work in an orderly fashion on the two of you. How's that?"

The girls looked at me and frowned.

"Lacey is worse than us?" Amelia asked.

I cringed. "I don't want to say *worse*. But that's because it's rude."

"Saying I had bride fever was rude," Erin said and then laughed. "Okay, you're right. I didn't realize I'd become a *Bride*." She said the word *bride* as if it had a capital B and was emphasized.

"You guys are great. And I know you're both really newly engaged and are having fun with it. When the wedding plans come, I will be right there for you. But please do not have me on speed dial, ready with text alerts that say 9-1-1 when it comes to bridal emergencies."

"We're not even close to the date. How does she have a bridal emergency? She afraid she's going to get a zit on the wedding day?"

I shrugged at Amelia. "Well, I'm sure that will come up too once we get closer to the ceremony. However, right now, she's worried that they're not going to have everything we need in the time we need it once she picks her color palette."

Erin nodded. "It's going to be a big wedding, and there's not a lot of time to get everything done with the big move right around the corner."

"Nope, but she's a drill sergeant, so we'll get it done. However, she's making me be part of every single decision. Even though I don't have an actual say, I have to be there for it. And I love my sister. I truly do, but I did not realize that I was going to be *this* much a part of the process when I signed up for this."

"Did you really sign up for it, or did she sign you up?"

"Touché," I said, and then the three of us laughed.

"All I know is when we get down to the nitty-gritty for your weddings, I am here for all the help you need. But please don't need as much help as Lacey does."

"We won't be that bad," Amelia said, then grinned over at Erin. "Maybe. However, we do have to decide on maids of honor."

"Please don't make it be me," I said and then laughed at the affronted looks on their faces. "I'm kidding. Just, you know, don't be Lacey if I am. I love her, but dear God."

"I'm pretty sure that you're going to cross-stitch that on a pillow for your house."

"Right?" I said at Amelia's words.

"We were sort of thinking we would do what the ladies of *Friends* did," Erin said, grinning.

"You mean Rachel, Monica, and Phoebe?" I asked, frowning, trying to remember the episode.

"Exactly. They all decided to be maids of honor for

each other. You just have to decide who's going to be first."

"That's actually a really good idea. But what about your sister? Or my sister?" I asked.

Amelia winced. "Yeah, we thought of that. But if that's who you choose, then we'll make that work, too. However, you said yourself, you don't like being your sister's maid of honor, what would happen if she was *your* maid of honor?"

Images of what had happened when Monica was Phoebe's maid of honor, and Monica had driven Phoebe crazy slid into my mind. "Well, Monica *did* get the job done," I said. Erin snorted.

"Your sister's going to drive you crazy. I love her just like you do, but..." Erin trailed off, and I shook my head.

"You barely even know her."

"Okay, fine. I *like* her. She's a great girl. However, you told me yourself that she would be too much for you."

That was true, but I did feel kind of bad. "And I know she only picked me to be her maid of honor because she knows she can walk all over me. She's my baby sister." And she had almost died. But I didn't mention that. However, the girls knew. "So, I guess you're right, I wouldn't want my sister to be my maid of honor." And now I felt like a heel.

"And I already talked to my sister about it. She's far

too busy with the girls and life anyway. And she's pregnant again." Erin grinned at the word, and I clapped my hands.

"Really?"

"Yes. She's due right around the wedding if we go with the date Devin and I were thinking of picking. I told her we could wait, but she nixed that idea quickly. She asked if she could sit rather than stand. Mostly because she's been on bed rest with the other babies, and we're worried."

"That makes total sense." I paused. "She'll be okay, though, right?"

"That's the plan." Erin frowned. "My sister is the strongest person I know. So, yes, she'll be fine. But I don't want to put any undue stress on her and the baby. She will be a matron of honor in spirit, but will not be part of the wedding party. I want you two to be. Is that okay?"

"I think that's perfect." I reached out and squeezed her hand while keeping my other clasped tightly around the bouquet.

"And," Amelia said, cutting in, "since you're super busy on Lacey's, I figured I should be Erin's maid of honor first because her day is coming up before mine. And then you can be mine, and Erin can be yours."

"That sounds wonderful," I said, and the girls clapped again. Brides. "Except for the fact that I'm not engaged. Meaning we may have to wait a long time for that."

Or, you know, eternity.

"You never know, we weren't looking for love when it happened."

I blinked at Erin's words and then looked over at Amelia.

Amelia raised a finger. "Okay, I was looking for love when I found Tucker, I just wasn't looking for him."

Erin and I couldn't hold back an, "Aw."

"Right? I love him so much."

Amelia returned to looking like a Disney princess, and I rolled my eyes and went back to work. I nicked my finger on a thorn, growled at myself, and moved to wash my hand. I cleaned out the wound, added Neosporin, and then went back to work. It was routine at this point.

The girls were sorting for me, both of them having taken their lunch break to help me with backup. I had a large wedding to do flowers for—centerpieces, bouquets, boutonnieres, and mussy tussies for the mothers. Lots of things to do, but I was getting it done.

Erin had already finished the wedding cake, at least as much as she could. She would work on the rest in the morning, the day of the wedding. Amelia wasn't part of this deal since they were having an indoor ceremony, and they didn't need landscaping, but we were having fun with it.

I loved my job, I really did, but the thought of weddings, so many of them all at once, was a little over-whelming. And it reminded me of the fact that, yes, there was an imaginary groom in my dream wedding.

Caleb. And I still didn't have a plan for how I was going to get him to notice me.

Maybe I just needed to be in his vicinity. Often. And with the way that Lacey's wedding plans were going? That was going to happen eventually.

"So, are you and Caleb working together?" Erin asked, and I nicked my finger again. How did the woman always know when I was thinking about Caleb?

"Damn it," I cried out and went to rewash my finger

"Having issues over there?" Amelia asked, tongue in cheek. They'd watched me stab my fingers countless times, so they knew I wasn't really hurt.

"This is just a thorny bunch. It's pissing me off. And I'm not really working that much with Caleb yet." I tried for casual, but the girls met each other's gazes. None of us talked about my crush on Caleb. They all saw it. However, they were good enough to lie to me about it. At least, they didn't lie with their words, but rather the fact that we all ignored it. And I was just fine with that. I had to come to terms with my feelings for Caleb on my own first. Which I was at least actively trying to do.

"Lacey wants to know more about what John has planned for his stag party, so I'm going to have to call

Caleb soon about it. And then there's something about tuxes that's on my to-do list. But I'll get there. So, soon, I'll have to work with Caleb often. But not right now."

"And you're good with that?" Amelia asked casually.

"Yes, we're friends. We're the group. Remember?"

"Yes, we're friends. That works."

I didn't miss the tone of Erin's voice, but I ignored it.

Because I didn't know what was going to happen next. I didn't know if I should. After all, I was jumping off the deep end, only I had to make that leap first.

And that meant I should probably call him.

Even if I was scared to death of what would happen once I did.

Chapter 5

Caleb

I SAT BEHIND MY DESK AND TRIED NOT TO VOMIT. JESUS Christ. Why did it have to happen now? Oh, yeah, because it happened out of nowhere. At all times, of any day. There were signs, things that other people could see, at least. I couldn't. I didn't know when the migraines were going to hit, but I knew they were going to be bad.

Today, however, it wasn't going to be too terrible. Felt more like a regular headache, and I could keep going. A friend of my brother's had migraines that were similar to mine from what I heard. Those that made it hard to even want to eat or open your eyes.

Mine were getting just as bad, but the problem was that they came with other physical symptoms. Add in the fact that I wasn't sure if what I saw was real... And, yeah. What was truth, what was fiction, what was an illusion?

It scared the fuck out of me.

Crippling migraines and something that could be far worse than a migraine meant that I didn't work with my hands anymore. I wasn't out in the field, wasn't in Alaska any longer. I was home. Back in Denver. Because I needed my family, my brothers and my sister. And I needed to figure out what the fuck was wrong with me. But no number of scans were going to figure that out.

At least, that's what they told me. They needed more information.

And I hated that I didn't have any to give.

My stomach hurt, and my palms were sweaty, but I kept going, working on plans for the next site. I had moved over to construction when I returned to Denver, thinking maybe I could work with my hands again. But I couldn't.

I had a couple of friends in the business, people that were actually now Dimitri's relatives, ironically. The small world that was Denver and all that. I wasn't working for them, but I worked in a company that worked *with* them sometimes.

Right then, my job was as an overseer, getting all the little, nitty-gritty pieces of a construction site for a large company going. That meant I had to see to all the details, deal with emails and phone calls and materials and all that shit. I was the one who did all the planning now, and I had experience with it. After all, I did a bit of this when I was up in Alaska.

And now, I was doing it again, only this time with a damn headache that wouldn't leave me be.

I hated feeling weak. But that's what I felt. Weak and like a fucking loser.

"Caleb, how are we on that account?" Bobby asked as he walked past my door.

I had a corner office. I made decent money, and I got to wear a suit if I felt like it. I got to get all snazzy with the clients, or wear jeans and a tee shirt and work down at the site. I loved my job, I really did, but right then, I hated that I'd had to move to this job because my brain couldn't do what it needed to do.

"Almost done. You need it?"

Bobby shook his head. "No, just wondering. I'm working on mine, but you're always better at overseeing stuff than I am. I have no idea how you can get all those details in your head done without having fifty spread-sheets open in front of you."

I grinned. "No, I just have five spreadsheets that are like master spreadsheets. Have you ever heard of a pivot table? It's like God's answer to organization."

Bobby rolled his eyes. "You know, you say things like

that, and it's kind of hard to imagine you in your last job."

"What? Are you saying that roughnecks and boiler-makers can't have a brain?" I asked, only a little serious.

I was used to others thinking that my siblings were the smart ones, and that I was just the dumb jock who worked with my hands. I didn't really like hearing it from a coworker who had seen my work, though. One who asked for help constantly when he couldn't figure things out.

It wasn't like I could change minds. I could only be who I was and hope to hell people understood. Even if I didn't really understand it myself sometimes.

Bobby smiled, a blush creeping up his cheekbones. "Not saying that. I'm just saying that I kind of wish we had eight of you so we could get shit done faster."

"Things don't go fast in construction. You know that."

"That is true. Hey, are you going down to the site to meet the new crew?" Bobby rolled on his heels—the man was unable to stand still. That was probably why he sucked at spreadsheets and focusing on the job at hand.

"I'm thinking about doing it a little later. Maybe tomorrow, actually. See what they're up to."

"I know the main guy we're working with is good, but I don't like the fact that he hired a whole new crew."

"It's kind of hard when the old boss kept fucking

things up, and that meant the crew moved to the two bigger companies in town."

Namely, the two construction companies that were related to Dimitri's family. But I didn't say that. I hadn't taken a job with the Montgomerys or the Gallaghers because I didn't want to use that connection to Dimitri. I'd probably shot myself in the foot because of it. Plus, working with the best meant that I got to *be* my best. Only I kind of liked working with a company that was on the way to floundering. I wanted to make it better. And I was.

However, that meant that I had to deal with the old boss's bullshit, and the fact that we had lost three-quarters of our crew over the past two years. We *were* getting better. Slowly. At least, I hoped so.

"Sounds good. Hey, are you feeling okay? You're looking a little pale."

Bobby didn't know I was sick. Nobody did. Oh, my siblings had probably figured out that something was wrong, but they didn't know that I felt like I was dying. Not that I was. Because I wasn't. There was no discernible evidence that I was. Just because my brain was on the fritz didn't mean it was the end of everything.

"Think I probably just need to eat."

"Did you skip lunch again?" Bobby asked.

"Yeah," I said, not exactly a lie. My stomach hadn't been able to handle food during lunch, and that meant I hadn't eaten. That probably hadn't helped the headache, but I couldn't go back now and eat lunch.

"You should go eat something, man. Your brain's amazing, but you can't get work done if you're hungry."

"True. I'm almost done anyway, and then I'm going to head out."

"Sounds good. But can you, you know, help me with this one thing first?"

I grinned and nodded. I'd figured Bobby was in my doorway because he needed help. He usually did. I didn't really think the guy was going to last long here, but beggars couldn't be choosers, and even though Bobby was slow on the uptake with some things, he was dedicated. And, hell, the company needed dedication. That meant I was going to help Bobby as much as I could because I didn't want the company to fail. And neither did our competition since they were good guys, too. Even though, sometimes, I really wanted to work for them rather than where I was.

I helped Bobby with his work and went back to my own, ignoring the throbbing in my temples. It would go away soon. It wasn't a full-on migraine, and I wasn't having hallucinations—not like that one time. It was just a little headache.

My phone buzzed. Thankfully, it didn't echo in my head. That was progress. Last time I had gotten a text,

I'd thought that someone was smacking me upside the head with my phone.

I looked down, and my dick got hard. Great, apparently, just her name did that to me these days. It hadn't always been the case, but ever since I'd moved back to town, it had been harder and harder to keep her safely in the just-friends part of my mind.

Zoey: *Hey, I need some info from you for Lacey. Got a sec?*

Me: *What do you need?*

That was a loaded question if I ever heard one, and I wasn't going to go there. Zoey was nice. Sweet. And not for me.

Zoey: *Lacey needs to know more about the bachelor party.*

I frowned, worried that Lacey was keeping tabs on her fiancé. Not that I had any right to be defensive, but I couldn't help it.

Me: *Isn't that John's deal?*

Zoey: *Yes, but she wants the details so she can put it in her notebook. Plus, there's a few more questions about a boutonniere? Not a hundred percent sure, even though I am doing the flowers. When do you have time to talk?*

My stomach growled, but my head started to feel better. That was a good sign. Why not make a possible mistake?

Me: *Tonight? Let's talk over dinner.*

There was such a long pause, I was afraid I'd actually made a mistake. A big one.

Zoey: *Dinner?*

Me: *You know, the thing that you eat, usually in the evening. I was thinking steak, but we can go for fish. Or sushi. Or something.*

Zoey: *Sushi is fish.*

I grinned. She made me smile more than anyone. Even my family. I'd never really put that together before. Huh.

Me: *When I think fish, I think of like cod or halibut. Sushi is sushi.*

Zoey: *That makes no sense.*

Me: *Probably not, but now I'm hungry. Dinner?*

Me: *We'll talk wedding. Get it all out of the way.*

Zoey: *You sound so enthused. But sure. Where and when?*

I thought of my favorite Asian place that had miso cod, sushi, and non-fish products in case she wanted something that had nothing to do with under the sea, and gave her the name of the place and a time.

Zoey: *Sounds good, but I should warn you, I'm in a grumpy mood.*

Me: *I didn't think that was possible, but I like grumpy.*

Zoey: *You've been warned.*

Me: *Deal.*

Warned? I liked that. I just hated that Zoey was once again on my radar. Because she was a friend. Nothing more. Though nothing less either.

And yet…I wanted her. Damn it.

———

Zoey

WHAT EXACTLY WAS I DOING? Dinner? With Caleb? Oh, yeah, this was totally part of my plan. You know, the one that didn't actually exist. Because if I actually *had* a scheme, maybe I would have asked *him* to meet with *me* for dinner, rather than having him do it so we could figure out what we needed to do for Lacey and John. But back to the fact that I didn't actually have a plan because I was too scared to write one.

There. I said it. I was too scared to write down a plan. Because what if it didn't work?

What if I figured out that he didn't really like me or only wanted to be my friend? What if he didn't even want to do *that*? Maybe throughout all of these years of him being in my life, it was really just a proximity thing. That he had been forced to be near me throughout our individual travels all over the world.

Because it wasn't fate.

It was just an unhappy coincidence that Caleb Carr probably didn't even put two and two together. He likely hadn't even realized that every time I saw him, other than when we were with family, he had another woman with him.

Even if he might not have been dating that woman at the time. I mean, I couldn't really call it a *date* between him and that girl on the beach when we were kids. Only in my childhood mind, it was *totally* a date. He had been dating that girl, and the two of them were going to live in a house of cheese and happiness and be perfect, and I was going to be the ogre in the basement. I didn't know why I thought I'd be in their basement, but I was eight, I couldn't really help the places my mind went.

And it wasn't easy that Caleb had really good taste in women. I had liked every single woman or girl I had seen him with over the years. Every one. Even if I'd only glimpsed some of them from afar.

They were sweet, polite, not at all snarky or evil like the movies or books would likely portray them. They had just been good women that Caleb had been with, and they hadn't made me feel small or useless. Maybe it was because they didn't think I had any chance with him, but I didn't think that was it. Caleb just had really good taste, and that spoke highly of him. That was probably why I liked him so much.

And I really needed to stop worrying. Because this could be considered part of my plan. Even if he was the one to ask me out. Therefore, this could be part of our future. Not that I knew what our future could actually be, but I wanted to try. So, I quickly washed my hands again, wincing at the tugging of those open wounds on my fingers. No amount of Neosporin was going to help me from scarring. Roses had thorns, and so did my future.

Maybe I needed to get those words tattooed on myself.

I grinned, thinking exactly how overdramatic that was. I couldn't help it. I loved flowers and romance, and that meant I had overdramatic thoughts of how they entwined themselves in my life.

I quickly slid my hands down my sweater dress and leggings, hoping I didn't look too ridiculous. It's what I had worn under my apron all day. Hopefully, it looked fine. I didn't have any dirt stains that I could see, so I counted that as a win. Plus, this wasn't a date, it was just a dinner to talk about another wedding. Not mine. So, everything was fine. I was fine.

And I really needed to stop saying the word *fine*.

I hobbled over to the restaurant, my back hurting from being bent over the counter all day. I couldn't help but smile at the way Caleb had joked with me about fish versus sushi over texts. It was a silly thing, and everything felt normal. And it *was* normal. Just because I had an irrational crush on him that I wanted to actually make reality didn't mean we couldn't still remain friends.

Because we *were* friends. Had been for as long as I could remember.

I'd been in Caleb's orbit longer than I had been in Amelia's, especially if I went into the small details. I was a couple of years older than Amelia, and that meant it hadn't been until later that Amelia and I had truly become friends.

Caleb? We'd always been near each other. In the vicinity. Our part of the cosmos. We were the same age, after all. Had been in the same classes, walked the same halls.

We'd always been in each other's lives. Only he didn't know how I felt. I knew that for sure. If he had, he might've either run screaming...or done something about it. At least, I would like to think the latter could have happened. Or maybe I needed him to *not* know so he could find me on his own. Or perhaps I should stop thinking with my head in the clouds.

I turned the corner and made my way to the front of the restaurant. Caleb was already there, his hands in his suit pants' pockets, the sleeves of his dress shirt rolled up to his elbows. That only showcased his forearms, and I couldn't help but hold back a swoon. There was something sexy as hell about a man's forearms. And I had no idea why. They were just forearms. But the way Caleb's looked, all toned and tanned and muscly...

I let those thoughts trail off in my head and did my

best not to think them at all. Because there was no way I was going to drool over Caleb Carr. At least, not anymore.

"You're here," Caleb said, reaching over to give me a hug. I sank into him and did my best not to inhale his scent. I didn't want to cross over into stalker territory.

I smiled. "Of course, I am. It's for Lacey and John, after all."

Liar.

"So, sushi?" he asked as we made our way in. He held up two fingers for the hostess, who grinned at him with wide eyes. She bit her lip as she raked her gaze over Caleb.

I was doing the same thing, so I couldn't really blame her.

We took a seat near a window, and I looked over the menu. "To finally answer your question, sushi sounds amazing. And maybe you'd like some spring rolls in the middle for us to share?"

"Oh, and they have that yakitori on a stick thing. I think I could just eat a whole truckload of everything."

"Really?"

"Yeah, I haven't been hungry all day, but now I'm starving," he answered, not clarifying exactly why he hadn't been hungry. In fact, he did look a little pale, and I hoped he wasn't coming down with something.

"You want me to order for us?" Caleb asked, looking over the menu.

"You really think you can order what I like?"

"I know you, Zoey. And I know you don't like shrimp or crab, which is hilarious considering you love sushi."

"You don't really eat it either."

"True. Dimitri is highly allergic to shellfish, so I grew up not eating it around him."

"Oh, yeah, I vaguely remember you mentioning that."

He shrugged. "So, how about I order a lot of tuna, salmon, and yellowtail?"

"Yes, with like the red, crunchy bits."

"Oh, yes, the spicy salmon roll with the red, crunchy bits."

He grinned as the waitress came over, and he ordered a platter of sushi and two appetizers.

He didn't order any beer, just a water for himself, and I did the same. I had to be clearheaded when Caleb was around, and that was hard enough to do without alcohol.

"Okay, you ready to talk wedding?" I leaned back as I said it, reaching for my bag.

"Yes. I guess."

I pulled my tablet out of my bag and started scrolling.

"That is a lot of planning," Caleb whispered, his eyes wide.

"Don't even start. I swear, I love my sister, but she's insane."

Caleb stared. "John was saying something similar."

My gaze shot up, and Caleb's eyes widened. "No, not that she's insane." He laughed. "Only that it was a lot of planning, and Lacey knew what she wanted—or at least knew what needed to be done. She's really good at the planning thing. I swear. He said nothing bad. Only that hc was overwhelmed."

"I'm overwhelmed, too. And I know John wouldn't say anything bad about her. He loves her to the end of the Earth and back."

"It's kind of nice saying things like that. He gets so anxious sometimes that he walls himself into a corner. But Lacey brings the life out of him. You know?"

I smiled, leaning back in my seat. "You're right."

"Okay, wedding plans?"

I cleared my throat, forcing my gaze off his. Right. Wedding plans.

"So, bachelor party?"

"John doesn't want strippers," he said quickly.

"I didn't think he would tell her, but that's good to know." I made a note. "What are your plans?"

"We were going to see a game."

"A game?"

"I know it's vague, we haven't actually started the plans yet," Caleb said, wincing. "I've been busy."

"I'm going to just tell Lacey that you're still formulating, and the plans will come. Because if I come back with nothing, she will kill me."

"There will be a game if we can get tickets. And dinner. And probably whiskey. But not too much because John can't hold this alcohol, and I'm not a fan of getting drunk."

"So...whiskey, cigars, and some form of sports ball."

"Yes, but maybe not the cigars, because John again, gets sick."

"He's so cute."

"Yeah, he's adorable." He said the words deadpan, and I laughed, shaking my head.

It was nice having a conversation, feeling like this was a date even though it wasn't. I just *liked* him. We went over a few things for the wedding, and by the time the platter of sushi came out, I was laughing so hard I could barely breathe. I liked this version of Caleb, the easygoing one who paid attention wholeheartedly to whoever was in front of him.

"Caleb?" our waitress asked as she set down the platter. "I didn't know you were here. You should have sat in my section." She leaned down and bussed a kiss on his cheek.

He smiled up at her, and I sank back into my chair.

"Hey there, Ana. Have you met Zoey? She's friends with my sister, Amelia."

"Oh, hi there. I hope you guys enjoy your meal. Caleb's great, isn't he?"

Ana didn't touch him again, didn't lay claim to him, but I wanted to crawl under the table and die.

Friend of Amelia's. Nothing more, and apparently, a whole lot less. Of course, his ex-girlfriend would be here. Of course, there would be a woman near that he had been with in some capacity. There were probably a thousand of them lurking in the shadows, just waiting to pop up and say hello.

Ana didn't look the least bit territorial. She also didn't look like she wanted Caleb. It was just a hello, and then a goodbye.

"He's great. Thank you for the food." Did I sound snotty? I hoped not.

It wasn't Ana's fault that I had all this in my head. But what if we'd actually been on a date? Ana *had* kissed him hello. Something I hadn't liked. But, apparently, to the rest of the world, we didn't look like we were on a date. And we weren't, so the point was moot.

"Enjoy your meal, and let me know if you need anything. It was good to see you, Caleb." She waved and then walked off towards her section.

"So, did you want to go salmon or tuna first?" I asked, trying to change the subject.

"Ana is married. Ironically, I dated both her and her wife, Sasha—separately. I introduced them."

My eyes widened, and I mixed the wasabi into my soy sauce. "I didn't ask."

"You didn't have to. It was kind of weird that she came up like that. Even though maybe to a casual observer, it looked like we were on a date and not working."

My gaze shot up, and I almost spilled the soy sauce out of my bowl. "Yeah, that was a little weird. But, like you said, we're not on a date, so it's not a big deal. Anyway, tuna or salmon?" I was talking very quickly. Caleb studied me for a minute before reaching out with his chopsticks.

"Let's start with the tuna and work our way towards the end."

"Sounds good." And then I would crawl under a rock. Because I was jealous. Jealous of his past, envious of people who weren't with him at all.

And I didn't know what to think about that. Because I didn't want to be that person. But, honestly, what if we had been on a date?

We didn't talk about it at all. Instead, we went over the wedding plans and *only* the wedding plans. We ate every single thing on our plates, laughed and joked, and acted like nothing odd had happened. Maybe it hadn't. Perhaps that was all on me.

This part of the plan that I didn't actually have was not working out very well. We went out to the parking lot, and I pulled out my phone to call a ride.

"Did you walk here?" Caleb asked, worry in his tone.

"Amelia picked me up so we could go work out this morning, and then I walked here from my store. I was planning to take a car service home anyway instead of Amelia having to come back to pick me up. She has a date with Tucker tonight."

Caleb shook his head. "I'll take you home."

"You don't have to." Plus, being in an enclosed space with Caleb Carr probably wasn't the best idea.

We reached his vehicle just as I finished that thought. "In, Zoey."

I rolled my eyes at his growl but got in the car anyway. Bad decisions or not, I was going to save some money on a car service.

We talked about nothing important as we made our way to my house, just wedding plans and the weather. And even as we spoke, I wondered if maybe I had made a mistake. Perhaps I shouldn't still have a crush on Caleb. Clearly, he did not have one on me. So, maybe I should just get over it. Perhaps formulating a plan was a very bad idea.

He pulled into my driveway and turned off the vehicle. I frowned. "What's wrong? Why did you turn off the car?"

"I'm walking you to your door."

I shook my head. "I'm a big girl."

"And a big girl can get her ass out of the car as I walk her to her door."

"You're so nice."

"I try. Now, move it, Zoey."

I picked up my bag and hopped out of the car, wondering what the hell had crawled up his ass. I got to the doorway, and he was suddenly there, looming.

"What is it, Caleb?"

"I don't know," he growled and then lowered his head. My pulse raced, and I couldn't breathe. When his lips touched mine, I wondered if maybe I had died earlier and now this was my heaven, my torment, my insanity.

But then his lips pressed harder, and I was lost.

Chapter 6

Caleb

My lips were on Zoey's, and I didn't give a damn if this moment in time was a mistake. In this exact instant, I didn't care if the rest of the world surrounded us, or that I should have been focused on work, or what the test results would say if they ever came back.

I didn't care. Because Zoey's hands were on my back, her fingernails digging into my skin through my shirt, and she was kissing me with the same urgency that ran through my veins.

I hadn't let myself think about this, even though I'd wanted to for far too long. Hadn't thought I should ever think about this at all. But in this moment, she was mine. Her touch, her taste…all mine. It was an intoxicating blend that sent shivers down my spine even as I deepened the kiss, my thumbs on her cheeks allowing me to angle her head back. I needed more. Craved more.

She tasted of our desserts and Zoey. I hadn't known a person could have a taste.

How had I not realized that she could? That she'd have her own particular taste that would go straight to my cock, make my dick press harder into the zipper of my slacks. How had I not known that she would do this to me? That I would want more of this.

But as I moaned, and she sighed, I knew that part of me had always known.

Every time I had seen her when we were kids, or even as teens and adults, there had been a small part of me that always noticed her.

I loved being near her. Adored the way she laughed and smiled and blushed. She just radiated happiness, even when she wasn't all that happy. I knew that she had gone through hell when she was younger but came out of it stronger. She'd always had a smile for me. No matter what had been happening with the rest of the world, *she had smiled for me.*

She did so tonight, as well, and now, my lips were on hers, and I didn't want to stop.

Even though we really needed to.

I pulled away slightly, my breath coming in pants right along with hers as I rested my forehead against hers.

"We should have done that years ago," I rushed out, not realizing that I was actually saying the words until they were already out of my mouth.

"What? What was that?" Her words were breathy, and I swallowed hard, trying to figure out what to say. I'd had a headache before, but this was nothing like that. It was a whirl of words and thoughts that made no sense to me.

How had we ended up here?

Why?

"That was something we should've done before," I repeated.

"You kissed me."

"You kissed me back."

She pulled away from me, moved into the house, and started pacing in her foyer. "You've never kissed me before."

I slipped my hands into my pockets. "Did you not want me to kiss you?"

"I...I..." Her voice trailed off, and she blushed right to the tips of her ears. She shook her head, and if it weren't for the fact that she looked at a loss for words, I would have felt that unsaid *"no"* right down to my core. I think maybe she didn't know what to say. After all, I wasn't sure what to say either.

I hadn't planned on kissing Zoey tonight.

But damned if I would regret it now that it was done.

"I still don't know what that was," she whispered.

"I'll be honest and say I really didn't know either."

She looked at me then and laughed. Full-on laughed.

"What? What part of that was funny?"

"I'm sure you know all about kissing, Caleb Carr."

"Why did you say my name that way? Like both names were one word. A title."

She shook her head and turned away.

Regret filled my stomach, and I took a step forward. "I'm sorry."

She turned then, raising her chin. "Sorry for kissing me? Thanks for that."

"I don't know what to say. I didn't mean that I was sorry for kissing you. Because I'm not. But I'm sorry that I'm hurting you for some reason. I don't know what I did or said. But I apologize for how I'm making you feel. Or maybe even that you didn't want that kiss. I thought you did. Perhaps I read the signs wrong."

"You didn't read the signs wrong," she whispered.

"Good. Good." I was usually better at my words than this. But I couldn't figure out what they were. Even as I was speaking, my pulse started to race, and my head began to pound. Fuck. I needed to get home soon, or I would get a full-blown migraine. No one needed to see that, let alone Zoey.

Zoey.

What was I doing? Standing here in her foyer like I had the right to start something. But I couldn't walk away. Not now. Because what if I did, and it all changed? I didn't know what the answers were, but if I knew anything, I knew that if I walked away without saying a damn thing, I'd regret it. And I hoped maybe she would regret it, too.

"You've never kissed me before. Why did you kiss me just then?" Zoey asked.

"I guess the phrase *because I wanted to* isn't a good one," I answered honestly.

She stared at me, and I tried to read her gaze. I couldn't. "Actually, that's a pretty good answer." She ran her hands over her face and then began to pace again. "I wasn't expecting this. This wasn't part of the plan."

She froze then, and I took a step forward.

"What plan?"

"No plan. No plan at all. Seriously, there was never a plan."

"You have me intrigued. Was there a plan for me, Zoey?" Had those looks I had seen been real? Did she want me as much as I wanted her? Not that I knew exactly how much I wanted her. After all, I hadn't let myself think that far ahead.

And I shouldn't be thinking about the future at all. However, I was going to. Even if just for a little bit.

"I think you should go. Yes, you should go. Because that would be best for everybody. It's just…everything is so complicated, you know?"

She said the words quickly, and I shook my head. "I don't know if I believe that. Do you?"

"I don't know, Caleb. I thought maybe… No, never mind. It's a little bit too much honesty when we're trying to figure things out. You know?"

"I can honestly say I don't know."

"I wasn't expecting this. But I don't know. Caleb?"

"Yeah?"

"You kissed me. And I don't know what that means. As much as I really liked it. Because I'm not going to lie to you. I *really* liked that."

"I did, too, Zoey." My voice was soft, and her eyes darkened just a bit. I wanted to count that as a good thing. Though I wasn't sure it was.

"However, Caleb, now that I think about it, it's really tricky."

"Because you're best friends with my sister and with my brother's fiancée?"

"That and I'd like to think we're friends, too."

I took a few steps forward and cupped her face,

surprising us both. "You're my friend, Zoey. Since you were little. I saved you on the beach that one day, remember? All the way in Hawaii, of all places."

She blinked away a tear, and it surprised me. "I didn't think you remembered that."

"Of course, I remember that day. It scared the hell out of me that you could have died, even when we were younger."

"I would have been fine."

"Drowning isn't fine, Zoey."

"I would have found my ground. A way to keep my feet steady. I always have."

Wasn't that the truth? "Yep, you always have. I want to kiss you again, Zoey."

"I think I want you to."

As I lowered my head, my phone buzzed. She smiled against my lips. "You should take that."

"I should really ignore it."

"Your sister-in-law is heavily pregnant, and people rely on you. You should check it."

She pulled away, and I sighed as I tugged my phone out of my pocket.

Joey: *Hey, are you free tonight? I'm feeling lonely.*

I groaned and stuffed my phone into my pocket, making sure the sound was off.

"Let me guess, a girl?" Zoey asked. Her lips quirking.

"No one I'm going to answer."

"It's just ironic." She started laughing, and I frowned.

"How the hell is that ironic? I didn't ask her to text me."

"No, you never do."

"Hey, that's not very nice."

"No, it's not. But it's life. I think I need some time alone to process my thoughts. You should go home."

"I didn't ask for Joey to text me."

"I know you didn't. And you didn't text her back, and I was the one that forced you to check your phone. It's just irony slapping me in the face because I didn't have a plan."

"You're not making any sense, Zoey."

"I don't think I'm making much sense to myself, either."

"I want to kiss you again."

"I think I want that, too. But not tonight. We had wedding plans we needed to discuss, and we did. And we both had lots of work all day. I had an early morning, and I wasn't really planning for tonight."

"You keep mentioning that plan of yours."

"And it doesn't exist, so I shouldn't be talking about it at all." She let out a sigh and moved past me towards the door. I slid my fingers down her arm, and she shivered. "You should go, Caleb."

"I'm not going to her, Zoey. I probably won't even answer her."

"You should answer her. Be nice, no matter what. Having an unanswered text hurts."

"I've never not answered your texts," I said, worried I had somehow hurt her.

She shook her head. "No, you never have. You're always very aware of that. Because you've always been my friend. However, even if you're not going to go see Joey tonight, and I believe you because you're not that guy, you should still tell her that. Closure. You know?"

"I do. It just feels weird."

"Weird to close something?"

"No, weird to text another woman after having my mouth on yours."

"Well, there's nothing usual about us, is there?"

"No, I guess you're right."

"Thanks for tonight, Caleb. Dinner and plans." She paused. "And that kiss. Because it would be rude not to thank you for that, too."

I wanted to lower my head and kiss her again, but I didn't. I held back. Mostly because I didn't know if I should. After all, I had been the one telling myself not an hour before that this couldn't go anywhere. And here I was, kissing her and wanting more. I just didn't know if I had more to give. Not with everything else going on.

Even as I thought that, my head pounded, and I knew if I weren't careful, it would be past the point of safe driving. So, I gave her a tight nod and slid my fingers over her cheek, mostly because I couldn't *not* touch her just then.

"I'll see you soon, Zoey," I whispered.

"Yeah, wedding planning."

"And more. Because I'm not going to forget that kiss."

"Caleb, I honestly don't think I could." She smiled then, and I winked at her before walking out to my car.

My head pulsed, and bile surged up my throat. I knew I didn't have much time until I had to be home with the lights off. I wanted to think about Zoey, I wanted to text her and flirt and do all the things a normal guy would do. I just didn't have that option. Not with a migraine coming. A headache that could possibly be more.

Jesus, I was scared enough thinking that maybe the kiss had been another hallucination. Not that I'd had one beyond that first and only time, but I'd had one in Alaska, and it had scared me enough that I quit my job and changed my entire career.

Doctors couldn't find a single damn thing wrong with me, and I think that scared me more than anything.

I made my way home and threw up on the tile floor in my foyer. I cursed, crawled to the kitchen so I could get my cleaning supplies, only the scents and motions made me throw up again.

Jesus.

I couldn't do this. I couldn't do this alone. All thoughts of Zoey fled, mostly because I knew if I wanted to think about her, I would just screw things up even more.

So, I got out my phone and called my big brother. I needed him. My body hurt, and I needed my big brother. I wasn't paying attention when I called, so Dimitri was the one who answered, not the one closer in terms of geography.

"Hey." I wasn't even sure I was speaking aloud at this point.

"Caleb? What's wrong."

"Can you come over?" My voice sounded like I had swallowed marbles, and I coughed. "Need some help."

"Thea and I were just leaving Devin's after dinner. We're actually pretty close. Need me to bring Devin over?"

"You need us to call 9-1-1?" Thea asked, and I could tell that they were using the Bluetooth in their car.

"No, just need you. Use your key."

And then I hung up, closed my eyes, and used the coolness of the tile floor against my cheek to slow my breathing.

"Oh, fuck," I heard Dimitri say as he walked in. I hadn't even realized any time had passed. Shit.

"I'll start cleaning. Do I need to call 9-1-1? I will right now." Thea asked.

"Is the vomit going to make Thea throw up, too?" I asked, my voice drowsy.

"I'm fine with vomit. And when the baby comes, I'm sure they're going to spit up a lot. I should get used to it."

I opened one eye as Dimitri knelt next to me, and Thea waddled closer. "I'm just going to clean up the mess, and Dimitri is going to get you into bed. And then you're going to tell us exactly what's going on. Okay?"

She squeezed her husband's shoulder and then waddled back to where I kept the mops.

"Thea Carr, go sit down. I will clean it up."

I loved it when my big brother got all growly. He loved his wife more than anyone—except for maybe their golden retriever.

"What about Captain?" I asked, my head pounding.

"Our lovely dog is sleeping and fine. I texted Thea's sister to come over and make sure that he had food, water, and see if he needed to go out. You know the entire Montgomery clan will be here if you need them, as well as all the Carrs."

"Just need help off the floor. My head hurts."

"Migraine?" Dimitri asked, his voice pitched low.

"Yeah, thanks for whispering." I didn't know if I'd be able to deal with anyone speaking too loudly just then. Or even in a normal tone of voice.

"No worries. It's what I do. I've helped with this before. But, Jesus, this looks pretty bad."

"It is."

I tried to lever myself up, and then Dimitri cursed under his breath and slid his shoulder under my armpit. I leaned against my big brother, and we made it to the couch before Dimitri let me go.

"You know, you're the biggest of all of us, and I don't think I'm strong enough to carry you in your dead weight."

"Weakling," I said, trying to laugh, and then I groaned. I knew I shouldn't have done that.

"I'm turning off all the lights," Thea said as she waddled around. I wouldn't actually ever tell her that she was waddling. Still, she looked amazingly gorgeous and hilarious with her big belly coming in like three full seconds before the rest of her entered a room.

"I'm going to put a couple of your smaller sheets on some of your lamps. I wish I had my scarves with me so it wouldn't look too ridiculous."

"Let her nest, and let me take care of you," Dimitri rumbled low.

"Migraines suck," I whispered, and Dimitri came back with a cool washcloth, wiping my brow.

"It's only migraines?" Dimitri asked. "Not that migraines are a small thing."

"Did a CAT scan. No tumors."

Thea sucked in a breath, and I hated that I'd said anything in front of her. I didn't want to stress her out during this stage of her pregnancy—not that anything was wrong with her, but I worried. "You don't want to hurt the baby, maybe you should go to the other room," I whispered.

"The baby is fine, you're the one I'm worried about."

I heard more than saw Thea lower herself into the chair by my side as Dimitri helped her.

"Do we need to call your doctor?" Dimitri asked.

I almost shook my head but then thought better of it. "I'm fine," I whispered again. "I'm trying to figure out the answers. I don't have them."

"We'll talk more in the morning."

"I don't want to talk."

"You're going to tell us everything that's going on. We're your family. You came back here for a reason. Let us help."

"I don't have anything to tell." I knew I was drifting off, but I wanted to get the words out. "Migraines, a hallucination, no brain tumor that they can see. We're still trying to figure it out, but so far, just these really bad fucking migraines."

"Okay, then," Dimitri said, letting out a shuddering breath. "You get some sleep. We'll figure out what to do later. Together. All of us. You're not in this alone."

I might have argued, but I couldn't. I really didn't want to. After all, I had come back to Denver for more than one reason. I needed to tell them everything, hiding things was just stupid.

Deep down, I was so fucking scared. Because what if they had missed a tumor? What if it was something worse?

What if it was a neurological disease that they hadn't figured out yet?

I wasn't sure what would happen next. All I knew was that my body hated my mind, and my mind hated my body.

I had no right to kiss Zoey. No right to take a chance when I wasn't even sure what would happen with me going forward.

I drifted off as Dimitri and Thea whispered to one another. I knew I was going to kiss Zoey again.

Because I wanted to. Because I was so damn scared of what would happen if I stopped living.

I was just so damn scared.

Chapter 7

Zoey

DAY NINETY-FOUR OF NO PLAN. PERHAPS NOT THAT MANY days, but the lack of strategy was still evident, none-theless. I didn't understand why this was so hard. I enjoyed planning. I liked making lists and schedules. The idea that I couldn't do such a thing when it came to my feelings for Caleb perplexed me.

In reality, it shouldn't have been so difficult. There *had* to be some form of feelings on his side of the equation. After all, the one moment on my mind for the past few days had been *that kiss*.

He'd kissed me.

Me.

How had that happened?

I knew exactly how it had happened. He had leaned down, taken my lips, and probably just like every other girl he'd ever kissed before in his life, he had been all in. And I had tried to keep up. Apparently, that was my lot in life. Trying to keep up with Caleb Carr. I just didn't know what to do. I had it in my head that I was going to make him fall for me, but now that he'd kissed me? I didn't know if I was really making the right decision. What if I was going all in too quickly and messing things up?

What if he fell for me just a little bit, and then I ruined it all?

I pushed those thoughts from my mind and knew I was worrying over what could be nothing. After all, it was only a kiss. I still needed to formulate that plan.

A scheme that might make everything worse in the end. But I would make one. Mostly because I had to. I really, really had to. I couldn't stand by and watch my life pass me by any longer. I couldn't be forever the brides-maid in an ocean of weddings—no matter that the weddings were a new part of my life.

I couldn't merely be the florist who failed at love. Not any longer.

I looked at myself in the mirror, tucked my light hair behind my ears, and nodded.

I deserve love.

"I deserve love." I said the words aloud.

If not love, then maybe at least liking. Because if I hid under all of my feelings and anxieties and worries for too much longer, then I wouldn't be the Zoey that I needed to be.

I didn't have to repeat those words, they were my mantra. However, I did need to breathe. I had had a crush on Caleb for so long that I'd almost forgotten what it was like *not* to feel that way about him.

And having those feelings inside me when I was trying to act like a normal person wasn't healthy. So, I was going to be myself and try to show Caleb what he was missing.

I just needed to get over the fact that there were probably going to be a lot of women in his life. A lot of them. Even though they all seemed amazing and were great friends with him still—or at least perfectly fine acquaintances—I had to get used to the fact that they would be coming out of the woodwork for the rest of my life, even if we remained only friends.

My phone buzzed, and I looked down at it and held back a groan.

Lacey: *Where are you? You're late.*

I frowned.

Me: *I'm not late. You said I had to be there in an hour.*

I had worked late, into the wee hours of the morning, finishing up some bouquets for a wedding, and my head hurt from lack of sleep. No amount of coffee and then later green tea kept me fully functional for the rest of the day. It hadn't helped that I'd had a daydream and full-on dream about Caleb over and over again.

"Why am I like this?" I muttered and grabbed my bag. I had been planning to get something to eat, but as my phone buzzed again, and I knew it was Lacey, I figured a protein bar and a diet soda was going to be my lunch.

Perfect.

Lacey: *No, I changed it. Didn't you look on the calendar? I made an alert.*

I crossed my eyes, took out the tablet, and looked at the planning software my sister had uploaded onto the calendar and apps. Indeed, there was an alert, but it hadn't sent a notification because I wasn't insane, and I didn't allow notifications on any of my apps other than for voicemails or texts.

Lacey wouldn't be happy with that, though, so I wasn't going to mention it to her.

Me: *I'm heading out soon. I'll be there.*

Lacey: *Turn on notifications. I know you're hiding from it. But there's so much to do. And I can't have you be the one who's running us behind.*

I love my sister. I love my sister. I love my sister.

And if I kept telling myself that over and over again,

I wasn't going to freak out over everything Lacey was doing. Because, dear God, my baby sister was going to drive me crazy.

I got in my car and drove towards my mother's house. We were doing wedding planning there since Lacey and John's place was in the middle of being packed up. Lacey was sorting through everything for what needed to go with them for the move, and what needed to be sold or donated. So, I knew my sister was busy with all of that, plus her day job, and the wedding planning. I did my best not to stress over it. Plus, I knew that my mother still worried about Lacey's health these days. After all, high stress and anxiety could lead to Lacey getting too tired. My sister didn't have the energy that even I did, even though I wasn't the most energetic person in the world. But that's what happened when you had to pour chemical after chemical in your body when you weren't even big enough to ride the Batman ride at a theme park.

Lacey: *Are you here yet?*

I snorted as I pulled into the driveway, shaking my head. Only my sister would ask that question considering that, no, I wasn't actually out of the car yet and wouldn't be texting and driving. I got out of the vehicle, and my mother opened the door before I even had a chance to knock or open it myself.

"Zoey," my mother said, disappointment in her tone.

"Hi, Mother, I'm here. Early compared to the time that I was planning on."

I bit into my protein bar, and she narrowed her eyes. "Is that all you're eating?"

"Yes, I'm sorry. I didn't see the updated time, not that I could have come anyway at that time. I was planning on eating during my little break between work and this. Sorry."

"I have some cucumber finger sandwiches if you'd like some. We were having tea while we waited."

Tea. And I hadn't been invited. But that was fine. I wasn't actually jealous. I had been working all day, my hands ached from the number of twists I'd had to make with the bouquets, I had a cut on my thumb that hurt like a mother, and I didn't even really like going to teas or doing them. It was my mother and Lacey's thing, while Mom and I had other things we liked to do. I hated the fact that I was feeling jealous at all. Because it had nothing to do with wanting to be with my mother or Lacey, it was the fact that I was here, and nobody seemed to be grateful.

And, wow, that was an ungrateful thought. I would push it out of my mind and just work on this.

"Thanks, I would love a finger sandwich if you have any left."

I leaned over and kissed my mother on the cheek. "And you look really wonderful, Mom." I was being truthful, she looked great, she always had. She tended to tell the world that she had aged twenty years back when Lacey was sick, but I didn't think so. I thought the determination and strength that soaked into her bones and her veins just made her even more beautiful. I didn't mention that, though, because she didn't like to be reminded. After all, Lacey was a constant reminder that we'd almost lost everything. And that was why I wasn't going to freak out and get stressed out over Lacey's demands. She was freaking out enough for both of us. I was going to get over myself and try to do better at this whole maid of honor thing.

"Thank you, darling. You look great, too. But what happened to your poor hand?"

She reached for my thumb, and I winced. "Thorn."

"Can't one of your workers take care of the thorns for you?"

We made our way into the house, and I could hear Lacey on the phone, her voice animated but happy. That was a good sign. "Not really. We all have to deal with certain aspects of the job. They're closing up the shop for me today since I worked so late last night. And I scheduled it that way so I could be here. I really am sorry that I wasn't here on time. I didn't get the update."

"You're going to turn on notifications, correct?"

I winced. "I hate them."

"And now you're whining. You're not usually a whiner."

"No, I'm not, and I'll try to do better." I said the word *try* because I really wasn't sure I wanted to turn on notifications. It was the principle of the thing.

We made our way deeper into the house, and I almost tripped over my feet.

Lacey was not talking on the phone. No, she had been talking about wedding plans with someone else. Namely, the best man. Caleb. In my mother's living room. Looking very, very sexy in a Henley with his sleeves pushed up to his elbows, and jeans that show-cased his very nice thighs.

I was going to hell. A very, very lovely hell with lots of my friends most likely, but I was still going there.

"You're here," Lacey said, cupping her hands in front of her. "We can really get started now."

Since Lacey's back was to Caleb, she missed the widening of his eyes. I did my best not to smile at that look because the expression of fear on Caleb's face was quite hilarious.

"Okay, I'm here. Sorry I'm late."

"No bother, really." Lacey walked around the table and picked up her tablet, as well as her large binder.

"Now, let's truly get started. Wedding planning it is."

Caleb moved over, and I took the seat next to him. I could have lied and said that it was the only seat available, but it wasn't. I just wanted to sit near him, and a maid of honor should be sitting next to the best man, right? Of course, that wasn't the case either. It was because I wanted to. Maybe this could be part of my plan. The one that didn't actually exist yet.

"Let's make sure that Zoey gets something to eat first."

Lacey frowned. "Why didn't you eat before you came? Or you should have come on time and had tea with us. Caleb had tea."

I looked over at Caleb and grinned. "You had tea?"

"I like Earl Grey. Hot."

I snorted. "Okay, Jean-Luc."

"See, I always knew you were my friend for a reason. Star Trek jokes and a healthy appetite."

My brows rose, but then I didn't really know what to say to that as my mother handed me a glass of iced tea and a plate of sandwiches.

"I know you're not a huge fan of tea all the time, so I didn't bother heating any up. I can if you want."

I shook my head. "No, I had green tea earlier, but I could really use the caffeine in this. Don't go to any more trouble. Thank you." I set everything down on the coffee table and started munching as Lacey began.

"Okay, troops, this is the point of progress for the day."

I risked a glance at Caleb. I had to look away quickly as his lips started to twitch.

I would not laugh. But seriously, *troops*? Yeah, this was going to be an interesting day.

"So, John really wanted to be here, but he's working, though it's fine, I'll put everything up on the planning page for him so he knows what's going on."

"Good, that means I won't have to try and remember everything."

Lacey glared at Caleb for that comment before she smiled sweetly. "I hope you remember anyway. That way, you can be a springboard for any questions he has."

"I would assume that would be a job for you," Caleb retorted, and I just kept eating, not wanting to be a part of this. It was quite hilarious watching someone actually stand up to Lacey during the wedding process.

"We can all work together. That's why we're here, after all. And now that everybody's here on time, we can truly begin."

I ignored that little swipe because, frankly, I *had* been on time. The time that had been listed up until two this morning.

"Okay, so we need to go over when the fitting times will be, as well as the wedding reception, and the rehearsal."

"Am I supposed to be taking notes?" Caleb asked.

Lacey's eyes widened, and my mother opened her

mouth to speak, but I shoved a piece of sandwich right into Caleb's mouth before he could say anything else.

"Eat that and take notes." He glared at me and chewed. "I know this is a lot of estrogen for you, but you can get it done."

He swallowed hard and then kept his gaze on me as he reached over and took the tea from the table. He drank it, not even asking if he could have any of my drink.

I did not know why that was so damn sexy. I was losing my mind.

"Do I need paper?"

"Use your tablet," I ground out.

He raised a brow and took another sip of my tea before setting the glass down and picking up his tablet. "Okay, then, let me know what I can do."

"You're going to regret saying that," I whispered, and I knew my mother had heard. Thankfully, she didn't say anything, because Lacey had begun again.

After my sister got through the intro, I held back a groan. Seriously, it was going to be a long two hours.

Two and a half hours into the meeting, I really had to pee. Two glasses of iced tea on top of the coffee and green tea and diet soda I'd had earlier made for a very stressful meeting.

"I'm so sorry, I really have to use the restroom."

Lacey sighed and rolled her shoulders back. "Yes,

we're probably at the halfway point right now, so it's a good time to take a break."

I boggled. "Um, halfway point?" I asked.

"We have a lot to go over today."

Caleb cleared his throat. "As much as I'd like to stay for the whole thing, I have some work to do. Can you put the rest on the tablet?"

"Of course, Caleb," Lacey said, and my mouth dropped open.

Really? He was allowed to leave with a simple question like that? And I looked like I was committing sins for wanting to leave. My sister had truly gone and lost her mind.

Before I could say anything—not that I would—my bladder reminded me that I really did have to go. I scrambled off to the restroom and took care of business as quickly as I could. Maybe if I was lucky, I could sneak out the back, and no one would notice.

I washed my hands and was drying them on a towel when someone knocked on the door.

"I'm almost done, Lacey. I promise I'm not loitering."

There was a rough chuckle from the other side of the door, and I quickly unlocked and opened it. "Caleb?"

He slid into the room, nudging me out of the way as he closed the door behind him, the lock snicking into place.

"What do you think you're doing?" I asked, and Caleb shrugged.

"I really wanted a break because I don't think your sister is actually going to let me leave. I'm pretty sure she has the place surrounded with like wild dogs or something."

My lips twitched. "Be nice."

"You're the one being way too nice. You can't let Lacey walk all over you like that."

"She always has." I said the words, and my eyes widened. "I didn't mean that."

"I know you didn't. But you're sort of letting her do it right now."

"I don't mean to. I just…want her to be happy." I shrugged.

He brushed his knuckles down my cheek, and I licked my lips. "And she can be. She just doesn't need to take over your life to get that."

"You're here, too."

"Because I needed to talk to you."

I froze, blinking. "You sat through how much wedding crap just to talk to me? There's such a thing as a phone, Caleb Carr."

He smiled then, and my ovaries burst. Damn things. "I love when you call me by both names. Like a title."

"More like a curse."

He leaned down, and I swallowed hard, looking up at him.

"Caleb, we can't. This is my mother's guest bathroom."

"Just a little. I promise."

"A little bit of what?" I asked, but then I couldn't think at all. Because his lips were on mine, and I was holding back a groan. He slid his hands around me before he cupped my ass, bringing me closer to him. I could feel the long, hard line of his erection as I ground into him like a wanton hussy. And I loved it. I didn't care that I was probably making enough noise to wake up hell, or my mother, all that mattered was that I needed Caleb's mouth on mine, his taste mingled with mine.

I pushed my hands through his hair, and he growled, lifting me up ever so slightly. And when he gripped me harder and picked me up, he slid my butt right onto the counter.

"You have to stop," I whispered, but he didn't. Instead, he started licking down my neck, kissing, nibbling, and I spread my legs for him so he could settle between them. He ground himself against me, and I wrapped my legs around his waist, kissing him, holding him. I wanted him right then and there, even though we hadn't talked, and this sure as hell wasn't part of my non-existent plan.

But before I could do anything, before I could make another mistake, a knock on the door froze us both.

"Lacey? Is Caleb with you? No, that'd be crazy. He wouldn't be with you in a bathroom all alone when we're in the middle of planning my wedding, would he?"

"I'll be right out, Lace."

"You'd better be. Do not ruin this, Zoey."

My sister stomped off, and I winced, resting my head against Caleb's chest.

"Oh my God, why did we just do that?" I groaned.

"Because it was really fucking hot?" Caleb asked, and I punched him gently in the chest.

"Why isn't there a window big enough in this bathroom for me to crawl out of?"

"Well, first, you're on the second floor, and that would probably hurt."

"Oh, no, I would survive. Lacey's perfect wedding plans wouldn't allow me to die."

"How about being in a cast or horribly bruised for her wedding photos?"

"Okay, you got me there. But, seriously, what were we thinking?"

"I don't think we were thinking at all," he said, and I could hear the honesty in his voice.

"What are we doing?"

"I have no earthly idea. But I'm kind of enjoying figuring it out." He kissed me again, this time softly, slowly, but I held my hands back, gripping the edge of the counter instead of him. Because I knew if I put my hands on him, I wouldn't stop, even if we were in the worst possible place for anything to be happening.

Then he kissed the tip of my nose and walked out of the bathroom, adjusting himself as he did.

That was hot. And kind of mortifying. Because Lacey stood in the doorway, her arms crossed, and her eyes narrowed.

I hopped off the bathroom counter and quickly righted my clothing.

"Hey, I'll be right out."

"You know what, don't bother. I'm sure it was a long enough day for you already if you've gone and lost your senses like this."

I turned to her, my eyes wide. "I thought you wanted me to spend time with Caleb."

Not exactly the words I was thinking, but they were the truth. My sister had been the matchmaker at first, after all. What had changed?

"For you to be cute and sweet with each other. Not paw at each other and practically have sex in Mom's bathroom. Thankfully, she's outside on the phone with Dad, talking about something. Seriously, do not ruin this, Zoey. This is my wedding. This is supposed to be the happiest day of my life. Don't make it about you." Lacey stomped off again, and I just stood there staring at her retreating form, blinking.

What in the ever-loving hell? Since when had I made anything about me?

I fisted my hands at my sides and tried to control my breathing.

I loved my sister. Lacey was a huge part of me. I honestly didn't know who I was without her. But I still could not believe that she had just said those words.

Shame crawled over me because, yes, this hadn't been the place for what Caleb and I had done, and I shouldn't have kissed him or let him kiss me. But I hadn't thought my sister's words could hurt this much.

I slunk out of the bathroom, all heat and emotion from before wiped away with one quick, cruel sentence. I grabbed my bag and my phone and my tablet from the table and hurried out to my car. Caleb was long gone, and I was grateful for that. I didn't know what I would say when I saw him again.

What I would do.

Because I couldn't ruin things with my family, and I couldn't ruin things with Caleb.

I just hadn't known that my title and place in my family had become this.

The one who ruined.

Chapter 8

Caleb

"WHY EXACTLY AM I HERE AGAIN?" I ASKED, WONDERING why I had been asking that question so often these days. Why did I always find myself in places I hadn't planned to be?

Maybe I could get into an existential crisis at that point, or perhaps I could just blame the fact that everybody in my life was getting married and popping out babies. Every single fucking person.

Dimitri just raised a brow as he sipped his beer. "I don't know why you're complaining. You get food, you get beer if you'd like it, you get all the soda and water and juice and sparkling beverages that you want, and you don't have to actually deal with baby games."

I narrowed my eyes at him. "I don't actually have to play baby games, do I? Because I'm pretty sure there are baby games at a baby shower."

Yes, I was at the Montgomery/Carr shower. Not that Thea was actually a Montgomery anymore. No, she had changed her last name to Carr since there were already enough Montgomerys sprawled around the state—and probably around the world at this point. However, the Montgomerys hated giving up their name, so it was branded on every single invitation, and even on the damn wall on some printed-out banner that they had made. Apparently, there was more than one artist in the family, so they had hand-done the damn thing.

I didn't know why I was so cranky. Probably had to do with the fact that I'd had blue balls since kissing Zoey, not once but twice. And both times hadn't been just a kiss. That second time? Dear God, I'd almost fucked her right there in her mom's bathroom. I hadn't been that horny and idiotic about where I was making out with a girl since I had been a teenager.

And even then, I hadn't crossed that line. Apparently, I was losing my mind.

And that sobered me quicker than an ice-cold shower. I didn't want to lose my mind. I didn't want my brain to be hurting at all. I hadn't had a hallucination since that first time, nor had I had a migraine in a few days. But that didn't mean one couldn't come out of the blue. So, I wasn't going to drink tonight, not when I had an hour-long drive home. And I wasn't going to ignore any symptoms that might arise. So far, so good. But I still didn't trust myself. Not anymore.

"Okay, you're not thinking about baby games and being at a co-ed baby shower anymore. You doing okay? How's your head?"

I looked at my big brother and shrugged, stuffing my hands into my pockets. "I'm fine. Haven't had an incident since you came over."

"Good. Because you're going to tell me every time you have one."

I glared at him but I nodded. "I will. Promise."

"I'm surprised I didn't have to fight you on that."

"I guess I'm scared shitless enough that I'm not going to hide anything from you anymore."

"Fuck," Dimitri whispered before he set down his beer and held me tight in a hug that I hadn't been expecting. I let out a shocked breath and then released my hands from my pockets so I could hug him back. I was scared, and I wasn't too manly or dick-sure to admit it. I didn't want to be sick. I didn't want to be weird. And I sure as hell did not want to die.

My throat went dry, and bile coated my tongue just at that thought, so I pushed it from my mind, however broken it might be. I was fine. The doctors were going to figure things out, and I was going to be just fine. The fact that the doctor I currently had kept running test after test and didn't seem to know what he was doing might worry me, but it wasn't like I actually knew what needed to be done.

"You know, my friend who also has the serious migraines is here. Remember, she's marrying into the family?"

I frowned. "I thought her brother was marrying into the family."

Dimitri shrugged. "I honestly have no idea anymore. All I know is that she was invited because, somehow, she's connected. Their whole family is here. In addition to a few other families who married into the Montgomerys."

"I have no idea who some of those people are."

"You don't have to worry about it. At all. Just make sure that you watch what Thea's eating."

I frowned. "Excuse me? You want me to get between a pregnant woman and food? Do you want me to lose an arm?"

Dimitri snorted, and I shook my head. "This is a cheese-themed baby shower. You know our love of cheese."

"You mean your unholy fascination with it?"

"There's nothing unholy about cheese. Cheese is good. Cheese is life."

"Yep, how right that is, husband," Thea said from across the room. She was back into her own conversation before I could even comment on the fact that she had somehow heard that stupid cult-like saying from across the room.

"The fact that you have a motto with your cult means you may have a problem with cheese," I calmly pointed out.

"There's nothing wrong. Plus, it's a joke between us now. Hence the oddly themed cheese baby shower for a woman who's not allowed to have soft cheeses."

"Pregnant women aren't supposed to have soft cheeses?"

"Nope. They're allowed to have hard cheeses and some processed soft cheeses. I have a whole list, it's printed out on the fridge, and we almost put it on the invitation, but I figured that would be too weird."

"Weirder than the fact that you have like eighteen different types of cheese available, including dips and spreads?"

"I don't judge you. You don't get to judge me."

"I really have no idea where to start with the judging."

Dimitri grinned and laughed. "Anyway, we made sure that nobody brought any of the incorrect types.

They're all on the list of banned contraband substances."

That made me laugh. "So, if anyone hides the brie within the cocaine, I know that they're on the wrong side of the law?"

"You mock me, but she's been craving soft cheeses, to the point that I'm afraid she's going to sleepwalk right out one day and find herself some."

I just shook my head, my stomach hurting from laughing so hard. "Thank you for getting my mind off what the hell is going on with me because you two are ridiculous."

Dimitri grinned, his eyes wide and happier than I'd ever seen them in my life. "Yeah, I'm happy. I'm going to be a dad, Caleb. I still can't fucking believe it."

I shook my head and then leaned down to pet Captain's head as the golden retriever came up to us. Dimitri knelt by the older dog and hugged him close, slowly running his hands down the golden retriever's back.

"You know, you pretty much raised me and Amelia, and Devin a little bit, too. And between us and Captain, you've probably got this dad thing down."

"I might've started with piddle pads for Captain, but I didn't start with diapers with you three. It's all new, and it's a little daunting."

"But Thea's sisters have gone through this before. Same with her brother, right?" I asked.

"So have all of her cousins. I swear that family breeds more than rabbits do." He mumbled the words, considering that all the Montgomerys had keen ears and were surrounding us at the time.

"It's amazing how much they all look alike, too," I mumbled.

"Don't say shit like that. They can hurt us. Did you see that one over there? He's like six-five and built. He could probably break us with his pinky."

"And I hear that one is actually married into the family," Zoey said as she came up to my side. I froze, unaware that she had been so close. Which was weird, because all I could do was notice where she was lately.

She handed me a water, and I raised a brow.

"I got one for Amelia, but Tucker had already gotten one, so then I was standing there with two glasses. I figured I'd give it to you since your hands were empty."

I looked down at her and smiled. "Thanks."

"No problem. And, really, I feel like I can get stepped on at any moment with all these giants around here."

Dimitri laughed. "There's a few people shorter than you."

"Do you mean the children?" she asked, a mock grimace on her face.

"Well, I don't know about that ten-year-old, I think they are taller than you," I said.

"I am not that short. There are shorter people here. Adults. I'm average height."

"Average for humans, not Montgomerys," I said and winced when a Montgomery, one I didn't actually know, punched me in the arm on their way to one of the cheese spreads.

One of the cheese spreads.

Because, of course, there were like five of them around the house.

"And on that note, I'm going to check on my wife. They're starting the games soon."

I narrowed my eyes. "You said I didn't have to play."

"You don't. But Thea wants to play. Therefore, I'm going to sit next to her and help her smell random mushed peas and beans to figure out which one's which."

I gagged. "Why are baby games so disgusting?"

"I'm trying not to ask myself that question, other than the fact that I think they're trying to prepare us for the amount of bodily fluids that are going to be sprayed on me when the baby's born. And after."

I visibly shuddered as Dimitri walked off to join his wife. I looked down at Zoey. "You know, this sort of makes me not want to have kids at all."

She snorted, shaking her head. "But then you get to

hold your niece or nephew and smell their little baby powder head and hold them close and feel their little fingers wrap around yours. You'll fall in love. You'll forget the fact that they poop and they throw up and they constantly cry and they never sleep."

"Do you think that's just what the media tells you that babies are like?" I asked.

"You mean this is a conspiracy? Probably not. But I figure I'll see soon when Lacey and John are ready for a baby."

"They're going the surrogacy route, right?"

She froze, blinking at me. "How on earth do you know that?"

"John talks to me when he's nervous." I held up my hands after I set down my glass since she was glaring at me. "He doesn't talk with everybody about personal things like that. But he talks to me. Has for a while. I guess it came with the fact that we were out one night waiting for a storm to die down, and we talked about a lot of personal shit. But he doesn't blab about his and Lacey's life to most people."

"I hope not, because Lacey doesn't need that."

"John's the most amazing guy I know. You know that."

"I do, but I'm still overprotective. She's my baby sister."

"Since, according to *my* baby sister, I'm an overpro-tective asshole, I feel you."

"You did threaten to beat up Tucker."

"He dared to touch my precious, innocent, little sister." I narrowed my eyes. "And you should stop laughing so hard. People are starting to stare."

"Oh, no, it's just that you think she's precious and innocent. And probably going to be a virgin until her wedding night, too."

"She can stay a virgin always. Isn't that the way things are?"

"I'm totally not a virgin, bro," Amelia said as she walked past, Tucker right on her ass. He had his hands on her hips, and I narrowed my eyes. "Why do people keep surprising me like that?"

"Because you're standing between two doors, so people can come up behind you easily," Zoey said, laughing. "Plus, the more you talk about other people, especially when they're in the same room, the more likely it is that they're going to show up and scare the crap out of you. That's sort of how science works." I laughed.

"That's not even real science. Or even close to science."

"No, but it's karma. As for John and Lacey, yes, they're going the surrogacy route. But if John brings it up again, please do not let him think that I'm so eager to be that baby's oven."

I choked on my water, having taken another sip before I set it down on the table between us. "You, wait? What?"

She shook her head, laughter dancing in her eyes. "Yeah, that was my reaction, too."

"They asked you to be their surrogate? Wait, does that mean your egg, too? Ugh, that's way too personal. Sorry."

"They haven't asked, but Lacey's hinted. So, I have no idea what they want. I'll see what my answer will be if and when they actually ask, but you never know."

"You really would do anything for your baby sister," I said, awed.

"I *might* do anything for her. However, if she keeps pissing me off about this whole wedding planning thing, I might not."

"I don't believe you. I think if she asked, you'd do it in a heartbeat."

"Pregnancy scares me, babies scare me, what comes out of babies scares me. So, no, I'm not a shoo-in for that. And she has to ask first. Adoption might be key for them, you know that they want to save the world together and be the perfect family. Adoption might be part of that."

"Maybe. But, hell, that's a big decision."

"Yes, so I'm not going to think about it again. Nor am I going to think about exactly what your brother's holding right now." She closed her eyes, and I looked over to see Dimitri holding a diaper, smelling it, and groaning. Wincing.

"This is way too weird for me. Plus, all the cheese? I just don't understand it."

"I think it's kind of cute that they have such a detailed inside joke that it's burst into this entire event. Plus, I like cheese."

"But just don't bring up soft cheeses, or Thea is liable to beat the crap out of you."

"Perhaps. I don't know her all that well since she lives down here in Colorado Springs. Still, now that she's part of your family and Amelia brings me everywhere these days, I'm getting to know her well."

"She's family now. She's a Carr. Not a Montgomery."

"Still a Montgomery," one of the big Montgomerys said from beside me, and I shook my head.

"I have no idea which one that was."

"I don't think you're supposed to know. I think they all just answer to Montgomery and speak as one."

"We heard that," one of the Montgomerys said, and I was pretty sure that one was a twin.

"And on that note, I think I'm ready to head out," I said, shaking my head.

"You're heading home?" Zoey asked.

"Yeah, I've got a few things to do for work and an early morning. I told Dimitri I wouldn't be able to stay for long. But I stayed for some cake, and they got my gift."

"Do you think you can take me home?" she asked quickly, and I froze, my cock going hard thinking about being near Zoey for so long.

"Didn't you drive here with Amelia and Tucker?"

"Yes, but they're going to stay a little bit later, and I was going to ask you anyway if you wanted to drive me home. Or if you could. Or I was going to ask anybody who was going up to Denver early if thcy could. You know, work and all that. And wedding planning."

She was rambling, and I didn't understand why. However, I didn't really care. I was going the same direction as she was, and it was over an hour-long drive. Alone in a car. With Zoey. The woman I wanted my hands on, and the one I should really stop touching. Stop kissing. Stop thinking about. When I didn't know what was going on with my future, I shouldn't be doing anything stupid like thinking about having sex with Zoey.

And yet, that's all I kept thinking about. That and making her smile.

I held back a frown at that thought. Where had that come from?

I wasn't going to think about that now. Instead, I was just going to do my best and not be an asshole.

I could do that, right?

"Sure, let's let one of my siblings know that we're heading out, and I'll get you home."

Zoey grinned. "Thank you. I appreciate it. Totally."

"No problem. I'll always be here for you, Zoey."

She gave me a weird look, but then I went off to find Dimitri or Devin to let them know what was going on. Tucker was the first one I found, and he shared a look between him and Amelia before nodding and letting me know that he would let everyone else know where we were going.

I walked out to my car with Zoey, and we got in, doing our best to talk about nothing important.

The fact that we knew we should probably talk about the two kisses and what *could* have happened between us meant that we should have been talking about something more. Instead, we talked about the weather and what was streaming. And the new cast of *The Crown*. We talked about nothing important.

And that scared the hell out of me.

Because I could never tell what was going on with Zoey. Even though I really wanted to.

"That was a nice baby shower," Zoey put in when we were almost home.

"It's so strange that Dimitri is going to be a dad now.

In my head, he's sort of always been one, even though he's not even a little bit."

"Right? He has those dad qualities. He's really good at the dad jokes."

"I'm pretty sure he gets those off the internet."

"But the fact that he looks them up at all is a dad thing."

"Okay, I can agree with that."

"Caleb?" Zoey asked, and my hands tightened on the steering wheel at the way she said my name. Hell, I had a feeling I wasn't going to like where the rest of this conversation was headed.

"Yes?"

"What are we doing?" she asked, and I swallowed hard. Yep, I really didn't want to have this conversation.

"I'm driving you home." I got off the highway and headed towards her neighborhood.

"Yes, you are. But I was sort of talking about the kisses at my house, and the fact that we practically humped each other in my mother's bathroom. I think we should probably talk about what's going on."

I shook my head. "We're just...you know...being good friends."

"Good friends really don't know how their dick feels against someone."

"Well, I don't tend to think about that, but thanks for that image."

She snorted. "That's not what I meant."

"I don't know, Zoey. I like kissing you. Is that a crime?"

"Not at all. I just don't know what happens next. And I think we should talk about what happens next, shouldn't we?"

I frowned as I pulled into her driveway. "Zoey."

She shook her head and got out of the car. "Forget I asked. Seriously. Forget it. I'll see you later."

I cursed under my breath, turned off my car, and followed her. "Okay, let's talk this out."

She had her keys in her hand but was shaking her head. "No, I don't think we need to. We're fine. Let's just not talk about it at all. I'll see you later."

She had her hand on the door, and I put my hand above her on the jamb. "Zoey. Let's talk it out."

"I don't think you need to. I don't think I want to know the answer."

I hated the fragility in her voice, and I loathed myself for putting it there. "Come on, let's go inside," I whispered. She turned and looked at me, her gaze searching. I wanted to be man enough to say no, that we shouldn't do this. I shouldn't go in and talk to her. I should walk away. But I wasn't. Because I didn't know the answers, and I wanted to go inside. I wanted to touch her, wanted to kiss her, wanted to see what made her tick. That might make me a bastard, but at least I was a consistent one when it came to Zoey.

"Just to talk?" she whispered.

I swallowed hard.

"Just to talk," I lied.

Just to talk.

Chapter 9

Zoey

My hand shook as I filled two water glasses from my pitcher before putting the thing back into the fridge. I didn't even ask him if he wanted ice, but I didn't think I could handle ice just then. What if my hand shook, and the ice just rattled around the whole time? I was already going to have to deal with possible water sloshing out of the glass as it was. I shouldn't add any more obstacles.

"Water, right?" I asked, my voice breathy. Really? I was an adult. I'd been alone with a man before. I had been alone with Caleb before, countless times. Okay, not necessarily *countless* because we'd usually been near friends, family, or *another woman*, but I had been with him enough.

And we hadn't kissed every time.

Except with the way he was currently looking at me, his eyes dark, lids hooded, lips parted just enough that it sent shivers through me, I had a feeling I was lying to myself. Just like I knew he had been lying to me earlier when he'd said that we were just going to talk. Oh, we might be talking, but I had a feeling if he didn't leave right then, it wasn't going to be the only thing we did.

Was this part of my actual non-existent plan?

No, I didn't think so.

I really should have written down ideas.

1. Spend time with Caleb.

2. Show Caleb that I'm actually a really great person.

3. Be near him so my soul can be happy.

4. Truly figure out if it's just a crush or if I am deluding myself.

5. Get Caleb Carr to love me.

Not a very good plan. Number five needed a whole subset of its own and should have been the title of the primary plot, but I think I was losing my mind. As always.

"Water's fine, Zoey. You okay?" he asked, and I swallowed hard.

"Just peachy."

He raised a brow, and I held back a groan.

"Did I just say the phrase *just peachy*?"

"I think you did."

"I don't think I've ever said that before in my life."

"There's always time to start," he said, laughter in his eyes.

"You're laughing at me, aren't you?"

"Just a little. But not cruelly."

"So. Water. Yeah."

"You said that."

Again, laughter in his eyes. But there was still heat there, and it wasn't lost on me that he wasn't saying anything either. We were both circling around the fact that he was here, and I didn't know what would happen next.

I should have had that plan ready. But it seemed like that wasn't going to happen anytime soon.

"The baby shower was wonderful. I guess next will be Lacey's bridal shower."

Caleb shook his head. "I don't have anything to do with that, do I?"

I shook my head in response.

"No. There was already the engagement party, and thank God we had nothing to do with that."

Caleb grunted. "That was fun, but I'm glad we didn't have to plan it."

"True. There's the bridal shower, of course, but I don't think she's making that co-ed."

"Thank God."

"After, there's the wedding rehearsal, and then the ceremony and reception. And we're not planning the honeymoon."

"Again, I'm going to reiterate, thank God."

I nodded. "There seems to be an endless amount of work involved for a wedding. Let alone the life that comes after."

Caleb took a sip of his water and then set the glass down.

"There is. I figured if I ever got married, which you know is probably never going to happen, I would end up just doing a Justice of the Peace gig. Or maybe something in Dimitri's backyard. He's the one with the bigger yard," he added.

I let that little nugget of information—him never getting married—slide right through me. Lots of guys said that. Heck, I said the same thing sometimes. Didn't actually need to be true. And I didn't need to let it gut me.

It was just a *thing*.

"You can make the wedding anything you want it to be. This is Lacey's thing."

"Yep. And I'm glad that it's going to be over eventually."

"Eventually," I agreed. Though it didn't seem like it would be over anytime soon.

"What are we doing here, Zoey?" Caleb asked, and I froze. I'd asked the question before, and there didn't seem to be an answer. How dare he ask the same thing when I didn't have answers? I had nothing except need and silly dreams when it came to him.

"Drinking water. And asking ourselves what we're doing because we're not actually talking about it at all?" I said the last part really fast and as a question, and Caleb just laughed, though I wasn't sure there was much humor in it. We were really good about rambling about nothing important and ignoring the elephant in the room.

Namely, what we meant to each other and where this, whatever *this* was, could be headed.

"I don't know what to say," I said honestly.

"I don't know what to say either. Other than that, I really want to kiss you again, even though I shouldn't."

My heart raced, and my palms went damp. "I guess we suck at the whole talking thing," I said.

"We're great at talking, and even about some important things, but we're also really good about avoiding *the talk.*"

I was sitting on the couch next to Caleb, and he leaned forward to cup my face. His palms were broad, fingers callused, the skin of a man who knew how to use his hands, and I held back a shiver just thinking about exactly what he could do with them.

His eyes darkened, and I had a feeling he knew exactly what I was thinking about. "What do you want, Zoey?"

"I used to think I knew. Now, I'm not so sure anymore." That was as honest as I could be.

He nodded as if that sentence made sense. "I think that's my answer, too. Because this could be a mistake. You're friends with my friends. Your sister's marrying my friend. You're practically sisters with Amelia."

"But not you. I'm not your sister."

Caleb let out a rough chuckle. "I've never once had sisterly thoughts about you, Zoey."

I blinked at him, confused. That couldn't be true. Not in all of our lives. "Never once? Not at the beach when you saved me? And not when you saved me that other time?" His eyes darkened, and I regretted bringing it up. But I couldn't help it. Caleb was intertwined in so many key and small moments in my life, that I couldn't help but remember the little ones as well as the big stuff that had changed everything.

"I couldn't beat the shit out of that wave for coming at you, but I still want to go back and castrate the fucker who tried to get you into his car."

"It was a cab, and I wasn't going to let him."

"You'd better not fucking blame yourself for it."

"I don't. Not really."

"The phrase *not really* doesn't actually help me believe that."

I shrugged. "I'm getting better. I have a therapist for that."

"Good."

His thumb was still on my face, tracing circles.

"Let's get back to you not thinking of me as a sister."

"You're not my sister. Not even close. Because if you were, I wouldn't do this." Then he lowered his head to mine, and I let out a shuddering breath, wanting more, wanting his taste. I sighed deeply, leaning into him as he parted my lips with his tongue. He deepened the kiss, angling my head just a bit, adding a slow caress.

I sank into him, wanting more, needing more. His hands slid over my hair and down my back, tugging me closer. He pulled away suddenly, both of us catching our breath, and I met his gaze.

"Are we not talking?" I asked, afraid of what would happen next. Because I needed to know what he was going to say. But I was afraid. So afraid that I would be like the dozens of women who were made to feel good, always respected, but then never heard from him again.

"I know I should stop kissing you, but I don't want to. You need to tell me what you want."

"I like kissing you. I want to keep kissing you. Only I don't want to ruin everything." That was as honest as I could get because I couldn't tell him more. Couldn't say that I wanted him. That I always had. That he'd had a special place in my heart for as long as I could remember, even though he shouldn't have.

"Then we just keep doing this. We don't let it hurt. Don't let it mess everything up."

I met his gaze and wondered what I was missing. He sounded different. Not cruel, but perhaps worried. Why would he be worried? Even as I thought that, I let those thoughts slip from my mind and leaned forward to kiss him again.

This could be a part of my plan. To be with him. I didn't need a happily ever after, but I didn't know what life would be like without my mouth on his. Without his touch, his taste.

I can make this work, I told myself. I could.

"I don't want to hurt you," he whispered.

"Then don't," I said honestly.

He tucked my hair behind my ears and then nodded before kissing me again.

The kiss started off soft, sweet, a bare touch of the lips, a gentle swipe of the tongue. And then he kept going, moaning.

He lowered me to my back, and I ran my hands up and down his arms, wanting more. He hovered over me, careful not to put all his weight on me, and I couldn't help but find that sweet. Even as it was sexy as hell. He didn't want to hurt me.

"Tell me when to stop," he whispered.

"Don't stop."

He met my gaze then, and I tried to look as confident as I sounded. He must have seen something there, though, because he kissed me again, his hands roaming.

When he slid his hand between us, cupping me over my leggings, I groaned, arching into him. He smiled against my lips, still kissing, still touching.

I wanted more, and I wasn't going to get it on this couch, not when it was so difficult to reach him.

"Caleb, I can't touch you. Not here."

He seemed to understand my unintelligible words because suddenly he was sitting, and I was on his lap, straddling him, my hands in his hair as I kissed him hard, his hands on my ass. He molded, squeezed, and I arched against him, rubbing myself along his jean-clad erection.

"You keep doing that, I'm going to come in my pants," he groaned, pulling at my hair.

I arched at the tug, then kept going, kept rubbing, kept kissing.

His hands were under my shirt, cupping me over my bra, and I wiggled, wanting more.

"You like that?" he asked.

"I think I want more."

"I can do that. Anything you want, Zoey. I can do that."

I opened my eyes then, trying to figure out exactly what he meant by that, but then his lips were on mine, and I wasn't thinking at all anymore.

He slid up my shirt, and then I raised my arms so he could pull it over my head.

When his lips went to my breasts, and he sucked my nipple through my bra, I shivered, wanting more.

"Look at you with all this lace under that prim and proper shirt of yours." He blew cool air over the lace of my bra, my nipples tightening into hard points, and I groaned.

"I like feeling pretty even when I'm usually covered in dirt."

"I'm a lucky man, then," he said and then went back to sucking on my nipples, tugging down the lace of my bra so he could get to my flesh.

His mouth was so warm, intoxicating, and I wanted more. I pressed my breast more firmly into his face. He bit down gently, and I squeezed my legs tighter around his waist.

"Did you like that?" he asked, laughing.

"Yes," I said, not able to figure out what else to say just then. I had pretty much lost the ability to speak.

He kept tugging, licking, biting, and just when I was about to squirm, needing release, he arched his body up and rubbed against me.

"Caleb," I gasped.

"Do you want me?" he asked, and I nodded.

"I need you to say the word, Zoey. Because this changes everything. You get that? You need to say the words."

I met his gaze and nodded. I knew this would change everything. This was on my checklist. I knew that. And I wanted the change. I wanted this. And so, I nodded again and spoke. "Yes. Please."

"Okay, then, Zoey-girl."

He reached around and undid the clasp on my bra, and I licked my lips before he went back to kissing me and then playing with my breasts. I was ready to come, needed to, but he wouldn't let me. Instead, he kept playing, pushing me closer to the point of ecstasy, but not over the edge.

"Caleb, please."

I didn't know what I was asking for, all I knew was that I needed it. But he kept kissing me, and then his hand slid around to my butt and pushed under my leggings, moving between my legs. I groaned as his fingers delved between my hot flesh, slick, aching.

"So wet for me," he growled against my lips.

"Apparently, you do things to me." I had almost added the phrase *always*. I didn't want to show him everything, though. I couldn't bare my soul while I bared everything else. He didn't need to know everything yet. I just needed this. This was everything I had ever dreamed of, and it was only the beginning.

I didn't need to put anything more into this than what it was. But I knew I wanted this. And I wasn't going to have any regrets. So, when he slid his fingers between my folds and inside me, I screamed, my whole body shaking. He plunged into me, hard and fast, even as his mouth was on mine, his other hand on the back of my head, keeping me steady.

I came in an instant, clamping around his fingers as I begged for more, as I arched my body against him.

I was still wearing my freaking pants, and he was making me come like this.

I had no idea how the man had done it.

I was shaking, but as he slid his fingers out of me and removed them from my pants, he put them to his mouth and sucked deep.

"Oh my God," I mumbled. I was sated, but still ready for more. I reached between us, wanting to touch him, and he arched up into me, a lazy smile on his face.

"You think you're ready for me?"

"Feel sure of yourself, don't you?" I asked, and then gripped him through his jeans. He groaned, and I laughed before wiggling over his hips as I planted my feet on the floor.

"What do you think you're doing, Zoey?"

"Taking."

I didn't know if that was the right thing to say, but as he grinned at me and helped me with his jeans, even as he pushed his Henley over his upper body, I knew I had died and gone to a special heaven.

Because Caleb Carr was naked on my couch, his body perfection, that of a man who worked hard every day, with long lines, lean hips, muscles covering every inch of him, and a dick that was hard, thick, and currently pressing against his belly.

I swallowed, and he smiled.

"Like what you see?"

"I think I'm going to like it better once it's inside me," I said and laughed when he widened his eyes at me.

"Little Zoey Wager with the dirty words. I like it."

"Well, I do learn from the best." I winked and then let out a yelp as he reached out and quickly shucked my leggings from my body. I stood there naked, feeling exposed in more ways than one as he looked me over, his legs straddling me as I stood in front of him.

"You look fucking gorgeous," he rasped.

"You're not too bad yourself."

He had his hand on his cock, leisurely sliding it from the base to the tip, one stroke, then another. I didn't even realize my hands were between my legs, playing with my clit until I noticed that he was staring, his eyes dark, his lips wet.

"You going to come right there just looking at me?" he asked, and I nodded.

"I'd rather come on you."

"That's the sexiest thing you could have said," he growled. "We need to be safe, Zoey. Do you have a condom?"

I swallowed hard and nodded. "In my room." I dashed away before I could think better of it, needing to breathe. I went to my nightstand, ripped open the unopened box, and pulled out a condom. And then a second one, just in case.

I turned and ran smack into Caleb's very naked body. His dick was pressed firmly against my stomach. And I swallowed hard as I looked up.

"Oh."

"Didn't want to wait." His mouth was on me again, and then he took the condom from my hand, and there was a ripping sound. I knew he was sliding it over his length, but I couldn't focus with my lips on his.

And then my face was on my bed, my ass in the air, my feet on the floor, and Caleb's hands were on my hips.

"This position okay to start with?"

To start with.

Would it be wrong to come right then?

"Oh, yes," I said, my voice a gasp as his cock nudged my entrance.

"Good." And then he rammed into me, one hard thrust that sent a shocked sound out of both of us.

"Jesus Christ," he groaned. "I knew you were tight from my fingers before, but…did I hurt you?"

"Not even a little."

I pushed back, pulling him deeper. "Keep going, please."

"As the lady wishes." He thrust into me, once, twice, and then over and over again, my body arching for him, wanting more.

Just as I was about to come, he pulled all the way out and then flipped me onto my back. He was still standing, my legs dangling off the side of the mattress before he put my feet up onto his shoulders. And then he kept pounding, thrusting, needing.

He was very lucky that I was flexible because my thighs were on my chest, my knees up to my shoulders, and he was leaning forward, his mouth on mine, as he kept pistoning inside of me.

When he flicked his thumb over my clit, I came, unable to hold back.

He thrust again, this time harder, and I could feel him come, his whole body tense as he filled the condom, his mouth firm on mine.

I was sweaty, aching, and knew that this had been one of the best moments of my life. He slowly let my legs down and moved so we were both on the bed, trying to catch our breath. Caleb got up and took care of the condom, but I couldn't even open my eyes to see what he was doing. Instead, I just lay there, panting, my hands lazily stroking my breasts because I couldn't help it. Caleb had touched them, kissed them, made me feel more like a woman than I ever had before in my life.

When he slid next to me on the bed, I opened my eyes and sucked in a gasp as he slowly traced his fingers along my brow and my cheek.

"I don't know why we didn't do that sooner," Caleb said.

"I don't know why, either."

That was the understatement of the century. At least, for me.

"That was amazing," he said, and I was so afraid that he was going to say that it was a mistake. That this was it. So long, goodbye. Thanks for the bang.

"I had fun. We should do it again."

I said the words quickly, hoping he wouldn't break my heart.

Something passed over his face, and I thought he was going to actually do it. Say that it was a mistake and that it was time to go. But, instead, he leaned down and kissed me.

"I wouldn't mind. I like being with you. We can see where this goes. Are you okay with that? No promises. We'll just see."

I nodded, then kissed him again, my heart exploding and breaking all at the same time. Because I wanted this, this is what I needed. This could have been part of the plan. I just didn't want it to be the only thing we did.

But he didn't say it was just sex, didn't say that this was the last time.

And as he pulled me closer and held me, I thought maybe this could work. Perhaps I hadn't moved too fast.

But even as he held me, I couldn't help but wonder what exactly he had been thinking when his eyes changed. What secrets did he keep?

Because Caleb Carr was full of them, always had been. But I couldn't help but fall to sleep in his arms, wondering what would happen when I woke up. And trying to figure out if this had all been one of my dreams.

Chapter 10

Caleb

A SLIGHT TINGLE AT MY TEMPLE BEGAN TO PULSATE behind my eye, and I cursed under my breath.

Seriously? Again?

I needed to find different meds or do *something*, but we were waiting on results, and that meant no Botox shots or anything else that might help anyone who got migraines with the severity and frequency I did.

Thankfully, the pain ebbed after a minute of breathing through my nose, my eyes closed tightly to avoid the light.

I let out a deep breath and then opened my eyes so I could get back to work.

I'd spent the morning down at the job site, making

sure that things were running smoothly. We had a few new guys who had joined the team, and they were pretty good. They listened well and had experience. I just hoped to hell that they stayed for longer than the last guys had. However, since we didn't have our old boss, I didn't think that was going to be a problem.

"Hey there," a voice said from the doorway. I turned to look at Devin. My brother stood there, leaning against the frame, grinning.

"What is that grin for? And why the hell are you here?" I asked, pushing away from my desk. I stood up and stretched my back and rolled my shoulders. I wasn't good at sitting behind a desk for long, but I was getting used to it. At least, marginally.

"I was on my way back from PT and thought I'd come and see what you were doing."

I scowled as I looked down at his leg, and my brother just shook his head. Devin had been hit by a car a few months ago. He was doing just fine now, but he still needed regular PT sessions since his job required him to be on his feet often.

It made me sick just thinking about how Devin had looked when I saw him in the hospital after he'd been taken in, but I didn't want to think about that.

It reminded me of the time that Dimitri had been hurt, and I really hated that my brothers kept getting taken to the hospital. Just like me.

"Things going okay with that?" I asked, doing my best to sound casual.

Apparently, I hadn't succeeded because Devin just smiled. He had that look in his eyes that said that he understood, but I really didn't want any pity from him. And I knew he didn't want pity from me.

"I'm good. Anyway, I finished PT and figured I'd stop by. Did you want to get some lunch or something?" Devin asked, and I rolled my shoulders back, thinking.

"I picked something up on the way back from the site." I winced. "Sorry. Wish I would've known. I would've waited."

Devin shook his head. "No, I'm the one who came to visit you out of nowhere. No worries. You want to come over tonight, though? I'll see if Dimitri and Tucker can come."

"You're really going to let Tucker come over after he defiled our baby sister?" I asked, laughing.

Devin flipped me off discreetly, and I was thankful that he did. That way, no one could see if they happened to pass by the door. "Tucker is my best friend. Don't say things like that, though. Remember, she's a virgin. Pure and innocent."

"Considering that I said that phrase before to Zoey, I'm going to agree with you there."

Devin looked behind him and then slid into the office completely, shutting the door behind him.

"What is it?" I asked.

"What's going on between you and Zoey?" Devin asked, grinning.

"Okay, not going there." Devin's eyes widened. "And, sure, I'll come over tonight. Erin not going to be there?"

"No, she has a big wedding to prep for, and then she's staying the night at her sister's house so they can have some sister bonding time. Her sister's pregnant."

"No shit. Pregnant?"

"It seems like everybody's getting knocked up these days."

I paused, my eyes wide. "Wait, is Erin?"

"No, she's not." Devin laughed. "Though we're thinking about it soon after the wedding."

"No shit."

"No shit."

"Strange, isn't it?"

"That somehow Dimitri's married, Amelia and I are each getting married, and Dimitri's having a baby? Well, Thea is anyway. When did we all become adults? And I noticed you neatly dodged the question."

"I didn't dodge anything, I'm just refusing to answer. That's not a dodge."

"I think that's the definition of a dodge."

"No, a dodge would be if I didn't acknowledge the question at all. I acknowledge that it exists, I'm just not giving you an answer."

"So, something *is* happening between the two of you?"

"Still not going to answer." I didn't want to. Because I didn't know what was going on between the two of us. Yes, we'd slept together. Yes, I wanted her. But I didn't know where it was going, and I didn't want to fuck things up. Plus, I kind of liked it just being the two of us. Even though it would never be only the two of us when it came to our family and friends.

"You sure that's a good idea?" Devin asked, and I frowned.

"What about the fact that I'm not actually telling you anything don't you get?"

"I just...I don't want either of you hurt."

Anger slid up my spine, and I narrowed my eyes. "You saying I'm going to hurt her?"

"No. Jesus Christ, no. You wouldn't do it intentionally. But you do have a track record with women."

"Have I ever been an asshole to any of them? Left them wanting something more than I told them I'd give them?"

"No, you're really upfront about it. But the fact that we're even talking about this means that you've done something with Zoey. Are you guys dating? Talking?"

"Really not any of your fucking business, Devin."

My brother held up his hands. "I know it's not. Not technically. Hell, I like you together. I actually think you guys are a good match. I just don't want either of you to get hurt, like I said before. And not only her. I don't want you to get hurt either. You're going through a lot right now. I don't want it to get worse."

I let out a sigh and rubbed my hands over my face. "I'm fine. We're going to figure out what's wrong with me." If my doctor ever got back to me, that was. I didn't mention that, though. "We'll figure out what meds I need, and along the way, I don't know... I have no idea what's going on with me and Zoey. We're not at that point yet."

We'd slept together, but we hadn't really talked about anything more than just seeing what happened. I was usually better about planning my expectations, as well as my dates. Still, with Zoey, it was a little bit harder.

And I didn't really want to dwell on the *why* of that.

I brought myself back to the present conversation. "I just don't understand how you actually think that Zoey and I are up to anything."

"I saw you at the baby shower. We all did."

I cursed under my breath. "Great."

"You never would've been able to hide it from us. And I hope to hell that you don't really want to. She deserves better than that. *You* deserve more than that."

Jesus. "I'm figuring it out. Somehow. I'll see you tonight for dinner, okay? Need me to bring anything?"

"I'm ordering wings, and I'll have drinks and everything. If you want dessert, though, you can pick some up."

"Aren't you married to a baker and a cake decorator?"

"I'm engaged to one, yes. But she's busy, like I said, and if I asked her for dessert when she's this busy, I'd get my hand slapped."

"Really? Ball and chain so quickly?" I winked as I said it, so he knew I was joking.

"First, fuck you. Second, fuck you more. Third, she's just really stressed right now, and I don't want to bug her. She'd do it in an instant, and because of that, I'm not going to annoy her."

"She's good for you."

"I think so, too." A far-away smile slid over my brother's face, and I wondered if I'd ever find that. If I ever needed it. Or wanted it. "I hope I'm good for her, too. You know?"

"I think so. However, I think it's her opinion that you're going to need. Not mine."

"That is true. Okay, I'm off. I'll see you tonight. And I'm sorry I pissed you off."

"You didn't piss me off," I said, hoping that what I said was honest. "I just have a lot on my mind right now."

"Tell me about it."

Devin headed out, and I stood there for a second,

staring at the open doorway, wondering what the hell I was doing.

I needed to do better with this. Be better at what I was thinking, figuring out what needed to happen. Only I didn't know what I wanted with Zoey. And I was usually the one who knew. I wanted fun, happiness, and respect. Sure, sex was good, but I didn't want to feel like I was using someone along the way.

And I didn't want to use Zoey at all. She meant more to me than I cared to admit, and she had always been my friend. There was a connection there, and I didn't want to ruin that.

So, I told myself I wouldn't.

I promised.

LATER, armed with an assortment of cookies that I had picked up from a nearby bakery, I was on my way to my brother's house.

I didn't know what I was supposed to think about Zoey. I hadn't texted her at all today, hadn't even talked with her since we slept together. Sure, it had been less than forty-eight hours ago, but I was an asshole.

Maybe I should do something more than just thinking about her.

I pulled up to my brother's house and parked the car. Before I got out, I took out my phone.

Me: *Having fun tonight?*

Great, that seemed like a good way to start a conversation. I really wasn't good at this. And I didn't even know what *this* was.

Zoey: *Hey. I'm working late. And then I'm going to head home and think about a fancy baked potato for dinner. What about you?*

Me: *A baked potato sounds pretty awesome. Cheese, right?*

I had officially lost my mind, but I didn't really know what I was doing. I never did these days, especially when it came to Zoey.

Zoey: *Oh, I even have cut-up bacon that I stored in my fridge. This potato's going to be amazing.*

I grinned.

Me: *You're going to have to make me one sometime.*

There. That was planning a future. Around a baked potato, sure, but it counted, didn't it?

Zoey: *You're always welcome over for a baked potato. Or, I could make real food.*

Me: *What do you like cooking?*

Zoey: *Anything, really. Although I'm not the best baker. Thankfully, we have friends for that now.*

Me: *Especially now that Thea and Erin are baking more with Thea pregnant. I'm going to have to start working out more to lose the weight of all the baked goods I have in my system.*

I purposefully didn't look over at the cookies that

neither of them had made. Maybe I really did need to eat a salad.

Me: *I'm on my way to Devin's house to meet with the guys for some wings. Actually, I'm sitting in front of his place like a weirdo, texting you.*

Zoey: *You're not a weirdo. But have fun. LOL*

Me: *You have fun, too. Don't go too crazy with your potatoes.*

Zoey: *I don't know if that's supposed to be a euphemism or something.*

I laughed so loudly, I even scared myself.

Me: *No, I was just trying to sound smart, and now I'm an idiot. But have fun tonight, Zoey. I might text you later when I get home. Sound good?*

Zoey: *I hope you do.*

I didn't say bye, didn't say anything else, I just let those words echo inside me.

I got out of the car and headed towards the front door. It opened, and Tucker stood there, grinning. "I thought you were going to sit in your car for an hour. Everything okay?"

Since my family knew what was going on with me, I assumed Tucker knew, too. Amelia wouldn't have kept that secret.

"Wasn't a headache or anything. I'm fine."

"If you're sure. I can always drive you home or anywhere really if you need it."

"I think you work longer hours than I do," I said, shaking my head.

"Maybe, but I can make time."

"You know, you don't have to suck up to me to marry my sister. First off, she'd marry you even if we didn't like you. Second, you're a good guy."

"Thanks for that," Tucker said dryly as he took the cookies from my hands. "Nice, I love this brand. Just don't tell Thea or Erin that I cheat on them with these cookies."

"I won't if you won't," I said.

"And I was offering to give you rides or anything you need just because I like you. We've been friends for a while now. Even before Amelia and I got together."

"Yeah, but still, you'll forever be the guy that is marrying my sister."

"And I really don't mind that at all." Tucker grinned, and I knew he meant it.

I loved my baby sister, but she was a lot to deal with sometimes. Not that I'd ever tell her that. Mostly because she could kick my ass. Migraines or not.

"Nice, you brought cookies," Dimitri said as he took the box from Tucker. "Don't tell Thea. Not that I want to keep secrets from my pregnant wife. But for my sanity, I'll keep this secret."

"Pregnancy going well, then?" I asked, looking at Tucker as his eyes danced with laughter.

"I'm so fucking scared and excited it's ridiculous. However, Thea has passed the point of being happy and sweet and wonderful and has gotten to the point of wanting to murder me. I think it's a prelude of what's going to happen in the delivery room."

"Hormones?" Devin asked as he came in, wings in hand.

"Do not say the H-word. She will rip off your balls."

All four of us winced, slowly closing our stances and shuffling our feet. Devin cleared his throat. "Well, on that note, I've got wings, I've got sides, and I've got ranch."

"What about blue cheese?" Tucker asked, and the three of us Carr brothers shuddered.

"Blasphemer," Devin spat.

"You guys are insane. I'm really glad that I'm marrying into the family, though," Tucker said.

"You can't help it. You've always wanted to be one of us," Devin said.

"Hey, speaking of family. How's Evan?" I asked about Tucker's son.

Tucker hadn't known he was a father until recently, and neither had Tucker's ex. Everyone assumed that the kid was her husband's, not the man that she had been with before him—Tucker. The news had broken when Evan got sick and needed bone marrow. But, apparently, the family was working on making firm connections, and

Amelia was going to be a stepmother. It was pretty fucking cool, even if sometimes I couldn't get my head around it.

"He's doing much better. The treatments are working. Thank God."

"Good. That kid deserves happiness," Dimitri said from my side.

"So, wait, that means we're uncles," I said as it hit me. "I don't know why I didn't think of it before."

"Because I'm not exactly married to your sister yet. However, the kid's got a huge-ass family now."

"Bigger if he wants to include all of Thea's relatives," Dimitri said, laughing.

"Dear God, we're not adding all of them," I said, humor in my voice.

"Don't know why you're scared of so many Montgomerys." Dimitri shook his head.

"They should be scared of the Carrs," Devin said. "We're starting to multiply."

"Speaking of multiplying," Dimitri said, and I froze.

"We're talking about Thea, right?" I asked casually.

"I was actually thinking about you and Zoey. Anything you want to tell us?"

I narrowed my eyes at Devin, who held up his hands.

"I didn't say anything."

"A-ha," Tucker exclaimed. "So, there is something to say."

"Don't say a-ha, weirdo. There's nothing to say. We're just…seeing how things go."

"Do the girls know?" Dimitri asked. "Because I think we all noticed, but I don't believe Zoey has mentioned anything to them yet.

"I don't know," I said honestly. "I'm sure she will. We're not exactly keeping it a secret, but we're not going to talk about it either. It's new. We're figuring it out."

"Okay, just don't fuck it up because then I'm going to have to hear about it from Amelia," Tucker said, rolling his eyes. I threw a celery stick at him, but the guy caught it and then crunched down. "Would've been better with blue cheese," Tucker said.

"Like we said, blasphemer," I said, shaking my head. "And stop thinking I'm going to hurt her. I kind of hate that."

"I can't help it. You guys were all assholes to me, so I get to be an asshole to you." Tucker winked, and I reached for a carrot to throw, but Dimitri held my hand back.

"Stop throwing vegetables. We're adults here. If you're going to do it, throw wings."

"Don't you dare stain my fucking couch," Devin growled. "And we're not going to talk about women tonight. This is men and wings and some kind of sporting event. What's playing tonight?" Devin asked.

I groaned. "Are we that focused on work that we've forgotten games?"

Devin shrugged. "Work, the aforementioned women that we're not mentioning, and upcoming babies. Apparently, that takes a lot of time."

I shook my head and leaned back against the couch, munching on wings as we turned on a college game and just had man night. I didn't think things would stay this way, what with kids and babies and weddings coming, but it was nice just to be for a little bit. Because even as my head started to hurt again, and my stomach roiled, I knew that I had to hold on to what was normal.

What was sane.

And maybe, just maybe, Zoey could be that.

If, like the guys had said, I didn't fuck it up.

Chapter 11

Zoey

My hands were cramped, my back ached, my feet hurt, and I was pretty sure I was getting a headache. Might as well round it all out for a beautiful evening.

I stretched and made my way to my house. I hadn't planned on working so late, mostly because I had been forced to take a longer lunch than usual—if I ever *took* a lunch, that was—because Lacey had needed me for wedding plans.

I hadn't minded that too much, though, because she'd needed to meet with the owners of the gorgeous farm that would be hosting the reception, wedding, and rehearsal, and John was supposed to be there. However, her fiancé had been stuck dealing with an emergency, and our mother had had a root canal, meaning I was the one who got to go with her. Mom was recovering, John was apologetic, and I was exhausted.

Lacey hadn't wanted to be alone, and I didn't blame her. There were thousands of tiny decisions that needed to be made, and she'd needed a sounding board, even if I didn't say much the entire time. However, that two-hour lunch ate into my day, and I still needed to complete the same amount of work. I was dog-tired, but at least I was done for the day.

And because I was running late, it meant that I wasn't the first one to my house for our girls' night. I walked inside where Erin and Amelia were working on a charcuterie board and pouring a glass of wine.

"See, I knew each of us having keys was great for emergencies." Erin spoke as she walked over, handing me a glass of red.

I drank half of it in one gulp and sighed. "This is bliss. Actual bliss."

"Long day?" Amelia asked, taking a sip of her own wine.

"Yes, but a good one. It was just long. I guess wine and cheese is always an emergency. So, yay keys."

"Amen," Erin said and clinked her glass to mine. Amelia scrambled over and clinked her glass, as well.

"Don't forget me," she said. "To wine and cheese and girls' night."

"Yes, I need food. Anything. I didn't actually get to eat lunch." I took another sip of my wine and wanted to drown in it.

Erin nodded. "Welcome home. And, yes, food is a must. Considering that you almost downed your entire glass just now, let's get some food in you. We have charcuterie, but I made those little meatballs that you love, too."

"Ooh, the sweet ones in the Crock-Pot?"

"Yes, I even brought over the meatball Crock-Pot."

Amelia snorted. "I love how Devin has named it that, even though I'm pretty sure you've used it for dips before."

"Not anymore, actually. I had to buy a bigger Crock-Pot for dips because it's not just me or the girls anymore. Guys tend to eat a lot of cheese dip."

"It's cheese dip. Can we blame them?" I asked, laughing.

"No, I guess we really can't. Anyway, we have a Crock-Pot of meatballs, a Crock-Pot of that cheese dip, and bacon-wrapped pineapple."

My stomach growled, and I actually groaned aloud. "Bacon?"

"You know it."

I took a meatball and considered dying right then in meatball bliss. "I'm so sorry I was late. I didn't actually do anything to help tonight."

Amelia shook her head. "You had your house open for us, and if we drink too much wine or the guys can't pick us up, you'll let us sleep here. I'm not really seeing a problem." She shrugged.

"Though, actually, I can't stay the night," Erin added. "I can probably share a bottle of wine with you guys, but then I have to go." She winced, and I frowned.

"Is everything okay?"

"Everything's fine, but Devin and I have a few wedding plan things to start on before we start the real planning, and tonight was really the only time he could do it."

I nodded. "That's not a problem. I like that we're at least having dinner together. And, honestly, I'm too tired to have a full girls' night."

Amelia smiled. "Oh, good. Because I haven't actually gotten to spend a whole night with Tucker in a while. And he's off work tonight, oddly enough."

I frowned. "Well, now I feel bad. We can cancel tonight. Most of the food will save."

"No, we're doing dinner. We're going to share this wine, and then we can go home to our men." Erin looked at me. "And maybe you can call Caleb and invite him over." She winked, and I did my best to look innocent.

"Oh, wow, you're as subtle as a sledgehammer right now." I blinked.

Erin leaned over the counter. "We can't help it. So, come on, when did it start? What have you done? Tell us more."

"All I did was text you that I had dinner with Caleb. And, suddenly, you think you know everything." I rolled my eyes.

"We don't know everything," Erin said. "That's why we're asking you."

"Plus, we want to hear it from you," Amelia added. "And we all saw you two leave together from the baby shower."

I blushed. "He was just giving me a ride."

"Yeah? Or were you the one to ride him?" Amelia asked, laughing at her own joke.

I rolled my eyes but knew I was blushing right to my ears.

"Ooh, tell us." Erin danced on her stool at the kitchen counter.

"I don't know what to say." I looked down at my wine, wishing I had the words to describe what was going on. I didn't know, and that was the problem.

Amelia patted my hand. "Just start at the beginning."

I sure as hell wasn't going to start at my beginning. Maybe I could start at Caleb's. Because nobody needed to know that I'd had an unrequited crush for as long as I had.

It was embarrassing.

"We just started talking, mostly because of the wedding plans, and one thing led to another. We kissed."

"Yay," Amelia said, clapping her hands along with Erin.

"And?" Erin prodded.

"And we're seeing what happens."

"Well, what has happened so far?" Erin asked, filling my wine glass a little bit more.

I narrowed my eyes at her. "Are you trying to get me drunk so I'll tell you what happened?"

"Maybe," she said, laughing.

"You are horrible," I said.

"I am, but I learned from the best. You both did the same thing to me with Devin. We want to know what's going on, Zoey. Plus, it's nice to finally see you guys together."

I froze. "Finally?" I asked, and Erin winced.

"Smooth comment," Amelia muttered under her breath.

I swallowed hard. "What do you mean, finally? Is there something you know that I don't?" I asked, trying to keep my voice casual.

"Okay, I'll say it," Amelia said. "You know how everyone thought Tobey and I were together, or that I had that huge crush, and nobody really talked about it with me in the room?" Amelia asked, point-blank.

I winced. "I'm sorry about that. Don't talk about

things that make you sad," I said quickly. Tobey was Amelia's former best friend, and after an unfortunate evening when Amelia had professed her love to him, they'd ended up breaking off their friendship because of more than that evening, but it still hurt to think about, I was sure.

That was one of the reasons I had never done anything with Caleb. I never wanted to feel what Amelia had. I never wanted to ruin whenever sanity and peace I had. But I thought it was far too late for that now.

"Well, don't worry about it. I have Tucker. I'm happy. And, yes, I miss Tobey in my life, but I like the healthy relationships I have now without the lying that had apparently been happening right under my nose." She shook her head, and both Erin and I reached out to her. "I'm fine. Really. But I do better when I don't have to talk about it."

"I'm sorry," I said quickly, and she shook her head again, letting out a long breath.

"No, I'm the one who brought it up because it's almost similar. Everyone thought there was something between me and Tobey. There clearly wasn't, and I'm glad for it because I wouldn't have looked at Tucker and fallen for him like I did. Anyway, the group of us *have* noticed the looks between the two of you, and not just on your end. It's been happening for a while now. However," she added quickly when I opened my mouth to speak, "we don't want it to end like it did with me and Tobey. So, we're thinking happy thoughts."

My brain struggled to catch up. They'd known. All this time, they'd known. No, they only knew some of it, of that I was sure. They didn't know the depth of my feelings—I wasn't even sure of those. And, until recently, I was pretty sure whatever looks Caleb had given me that the others had noticed, hadn't been what they were now. Not that I knew what those looks meant at any point in my friendship or now our relationship—whatever it was —with Caleb.

"I want happy thoughts, too. I just didn't know that everyone realized I had a crush on him." There, I could be honest and open about that much.

"It wasn't just that," Erin said quickly.

"Really?" I blinked.

"Well, we always thought that Caleb might have a thing for you, too. And considering you two might be feeling something, whatever that something is, maybe we were right."

I laughed. "I'm pretty sure Caleb Carr has never had a crush on me."

Amelia snapped her fingers. "See, it's stuff like that. That was how we realized that maybe you had a thing for my brother."

"What on earth do you mean?"

"You always call him Caleb Carr when you're talking

about him. You never called me Amelia Carr, or Dimitri and Devin with their last names. Caleb was always special."

I knew I was blushing, so I ducked my head. "I think Caleb likes it when I call him that."

Amelia looked down, and Erin laughed. "Okay, we are being *very broad* in our definition of descriptions here. I don't want to know too much about what my brother may or may not like."

I laughed at Amelia and shook my head. "I wasn't talking about anything dirty. It's just when we talk, or fight, I tend to say his name like that. I can't help it."

"How long have you had a crush on him, Zoey?" Erin asked, her voice soft.

I froze, swallowed. "Not that long," I lied.

"You don't have to lie to us," she said, her voice soft. "We're not going to judge you."

"It doesn't matter when it started, it's the *now* we're figuring out. It's probably just casual. You know, just a little interlude in our lives where we get to know each other, have fun, and then we walk away as friends. Because I don't want to walk away as anything but friends. You know?" I said quickly.

Amelia's eyes darkened, and she nodded. "I know. Just don't do what I did and imagine the end before you enjoy the beginning and the middle."

"I did the same thing," Erin added. "I was waiting

for the shoe to drop, and Devin to leave, so much that I almost missed what was right in front of me. So, don't forget what's good and enjoy what's now."

They looked so worried for me that I was a little worried, too.

I just smiled and nodded. "I promise I'm not going to do anything stupid. Other than, you know, sleeping with your brother," I said quickly, and Amelia screamed.

"Oh my God, you slept together?"

"I thought you had already figured that out," I said, holding back a laugh.

"You hadn't said the words before," she said, wincing.

"So, how was it?" Erin asked, and Amelia clamped her hands over her ears.

"No, do not say that. I do not want to know."

"You can just give me a thumbs up or a thumbs down," Erin said, and Amelia screamed again.

"Close your eyes, you wuss," Erin said, still laughing.

"I don't know if I should tell you," I said, this time trying not to burst into a fit of giggles.

"Oh, you should totally tell us," Erin said. "This is what girls' night is for. Cheese, wine, and penises."

"Stop saying penis when you're talking about my brothers. I need new friends. Ones that aren't sleeping with my brothers," Amelia said.

"Oh, come on, maybe you shouldn't have brothers

with amazing dicks," I said, laughing when Amelia threw a throw pillow at me. I caught it before it knocked into the wine bottle and shook my head. "You're such a baby," I said, and Amelia flipped me off.

"I'm going to find a way to get you back for this. All of you." Then she closed her eyes, and Erin grinned.

"Okay, thumbs up or thumbs down."

I knew I should probably be discreet and not talk about Caleb when he wasn't here, however, I couldn't help it. I was excited. This was new for me. This was everything that I had ever wanted, even though we didn't know exactly what was happening.

So, I held up both thumbs, and wiggled my butt, grinning widely.

Erin laughed, and Amelia groaned.

"Is she making penis hand gestures or something? No, don't tell me. I don't want to know."

"You can open your eyes now," I said, laughing. "I'm not going to talk about how I defiled your brother," I said, fluttering my eyelashes.

"Oh, yeah, Caleb was totally a virgin," Amelia said, rolling her eyes. And then she froze and put her hand over her mouth. "I'm so sorry," she mumbled.

"What?" I said, truly not hurt at all. "Do you think I actually thought Caleb was a virgin? I have met so many of his girlfriends in my life, it's a little ridiculous. I could probably write a tell-all book, and it'd end up being five hundred pages long, and I'd still miss a few," I said honestly.

"Does that bother you?" Amelia asked.

"Does what bother me?"

"That he's been with so many women? I mean, I don't think he slept with all of them," Amelia said, wincing. "No, I don't want to think about all of that. However, I don't think he's slept with every woman he's been on a date with."

"Well, if he did, his number would be a little staggering," I said dryly. "But I don't know, I don't think it bothers me that he has a past with women. He's allowed to. And I've always seen him treat women wonderfully. And every ex that's ever come up to us recently has been sweet with him, but never jealous or rude."

"I swear, Denver's the biggest small town ever," Erin said. "I keep running into my ex, so I can only imagine what it's like for you and Caleb."

I reached out and squeezed Erin's hand.

Erin smiled. "It's fine, really. I've truly moved on. And you can't exactly change your past with Caleb, but you can look forward to a future."

I shrugged.

"I don't want to look only forward, because that's where disappointment can lie. I'm allowed to live in the moment and help plan three weddings all at once, and just have fun. I'm allowed to have fun."

"Yes, you are."

Amelia kissed my temple, and Erin kissed the other, and then we ate some cheese, drank some wine, and purposely did not talk about dicks. Mostly because I was afraid Amelia might actually hurt me.

By the time they left, I was full, happy, and thinking about another glass of wine. The doorbell rang, and I frowned, wondering if it was one of the girls.

I opened it and froze. "Caleb," I whispered, my throat dry.

"Hey there. Devin said that Erin was just getting home, so I thought I'd stop by."

"You didn't call or text, right? I didn't miss something, did I?" I reached into my pocket to get my phone, but he put his hand on my arm and shook his head.

"I thought I'd surprise you. Pretend that we're living in a pre-cellphone era. Like the stone age."

I snorted. "I know, how did people deal with others just randomly showing up on their doorstep? Or, God, using the phone for talking rather than texting."

I shuddered and then moved back so Caleb could come inside.

"I can leave if you want some time alone."

"No, it was a good night, and the girls had to go to their men.

"So, I guess your man came to you?" Caleb asked, and my eyes widened. He laughed and shook his head.

"We don't have to actually call me your man. Though, it's kind of weird. I'm not used to being all possessive like that. Who knew?"

He leaned down and rubbed his lips on mine, and I was so still for a moment, I thought this was a dream. The man of my crushes since I was a child was here, his lips on mine, and he was here because he wanted to be. He wanted to see me.

And I hadn't even asked him to come over.

How is this my life?

I moaned, and he leaned back, biting my lip gently before kissing the sting away.

"Well, we could Netflix and chill, if you want," he said, and I rolled my eyes.

"No one actually says that. We're not like twenty or something and trying to be cool."

"True, but let's watch a movie. I'm exhausted, and frankly, I just wanted to hang out. Is that okay?"

I swallowed hard. "I think that sounds wonderful. But if I fall asleep, don't make fun of me if I snore or drool."

He tucked my hair behind my ear, and I fell a little bit more in love with him than I should have.

"I promise. As long as you do the same."

"Deal. What movie do you want?"

"I guess we're going to have to fight over it." He grinned, took me to the living room, and I did my best not to fall. Not on my face, but in my heart. Because I couldn't love him as much as I thought I did just then. I couldn't let this crush be anything more than it was. I needed to go slow.

Because my plan that wasn't a plan was coming to fruition, and I was so afraid of what would happen once I let myself go and believed in it.

Chapter 12

Caleb

"WHY ARE WE CALLING IT A STAG PARTY INSTEAD OF A bachelor party?" one of the other groomsmen asked as I leaned against the leather interior of the limo we were currently riding in.

"Because it sounds better than a bachelor party?" I answered, shrugging.

"I don't know, this sort of sounds like we're all going to rut on each other or something," the guy said, clearly having had a little too much whiskey at the first stop we'd been at.

John sat next to me, his shoulders shaking as he tried to hold back laughter.

I just glared at him. "Hey, you need to deal with this. These are your friends."

John wrapped his arm around my shoulder and gave it a squeeze. "Hey, we can all be your friends. We all come from different walks of life, but we're coming here for a common purpose. The stag."

I narrowed my eyes at him. "You had one drink. *One* drink at that whiskey and cigar bar."

"I think the smell of cigars got me drunk."

"I don't think that can actually happen," I said, but John just shook his head.

"I like the word *stag* because it's British. Isn't it?" I stared at him. "Back in the old Georgian or Regency days, isn't that what they would call it? And I think they still do over there. Anyway, I wanted to sound fancy. And so did my future wife." John grinned. "My future wife. Don't you just love hearing that? Wife wife wife wife wife."

I held back a smile, letting John continue talking about stags and British people and his future wife. John was only one drink into the evening, and he was already a little tipsy. But that was John for you. He just couldn't hold his liquor, and that's why I knew John would be drinking club soda for the rest of the night.

I too was drinking club soda all night, but mostly I wanted to have my wits about me. Someone needed to be the responsible one in the group, I just hadn't known it would be me. When had that happened? When did I become the responsible one?

How scary was that?

I wasn't usually the person who held back and made sure everybody else was doing what they should, but you know, time changed a man. That and a possible brain tumor that wasn't actually a brain tumor. Yeah, that did things, too. Not to mention the fact that I was actually worried that Zoey might hurt me if I let anything happen to John. Oh, I didn't want anything to happen to John. But Zoey was so stressed out over everything that Lacey needed her to do, especially over the past couple of weeks when things had started to really move along, that I did not want anything to put her over the edge.

I didn't know when she had become a driving force in my decisions. Though maybe I liked it. Or perhaps I just needed to pretend that that wasn't the case.

"Where are we heading next?" John asked.

"The comic shop," I answered for the third time in as many minutes since the entire group kept asking. "Remember, you're the one who helped me make the itinerary."

John just grinned. "Oh, yeah, we get the whole night with comics."

"But no booze allowed in there," I said, glaring at

the rest of the guys. Be on your best behavior. And if you hurt any of those precious comics, you not only have to buy them, the two-hundred-and-fifty-pound muscular guy who owns the place might actually kill you."

"I could take him," one of the guys said, flexing his muscles. The guy was an actual bodybuilder, so he might be able to take the owner of the comic shop, but that wasn't something I wanted to risk.

"Or we could just not be assholes." I winked as I said it and sipped at my club soda as we pulled into the parking lot.

"You're no fun," one of the guys said, thankfully joking.

"Hey, we always need a sober one," John said, already less drunk than he had been before. It didn't take long for John to get drunk, but he usually fought through all of the booze haze pretty quickly.

"That is true. Never thought it would be you, Caleb," the drunkest guy said, giggling.

A grown man, giggling. How much whiskey had they had behind my back?

"Well, I'm just keeping you guys alive. Because that man could kill you with one hand."

"But, *comics*. I'm excited. Are we allowed to buy things tonight? I don't remember. No more whiskey for me." There was reverence in John's tone that made me smile.

"You can buy anything you want, but I am going to be holding your credit card," I said, shaking my head as John mock pouted.

"We don't want you spending your entire honeymoon budget on comics."

"I would never do that." The man looked clearly affronted, but I couldn't help but snort.

Tonight was an interesting night: comics, whiskey and cigars, and later, we would hit a dive bar, one that I knew well that actually had fun drinks and a good atmosphere. It wasn't what I would've imagined as the perfect bachelor party, but I never really thought of my own.

An image of Zoey in a white dress at the end of an aisle filled my brain, and I almost choked.

Okay, what had I put into that club soda? We'd only been together a few weeks, and we were casual, nothing serious. We couldn't get serious. Because I didn't know what was wrong with me. And even though I hadn't had a full-blown migraine since Dimitri had helped me that night, they could come at any moment. And I didn't want to fuck anything up. So, thinking about Zoey in a wedding dress when we weren't anywhere near there yet was stupid.

I had to keep things slow, casual. We had to remain friends who sometimes slept together and hung out and did things together.

Jesus, I needed to take a step back.

Things were getting far too serious too quickly in the back of my mind if I was already having weird thoughts like Zoey in a wedding dress. I quickly pushed those thoughts out of my head and waited until we got into the comic shop to try and catch my breath.

Zoey.

Wedding dress.

Jesus.

I leaned against the wall, watching everybody. I liked reading, and I enjoyed comic movies and TV shows, but I wasn't a huge fan of reading comic books. They just weren't my cup of tea, but I loved the way John's eyes lit up as he looked at all of them. It was like he was a little kid again.

Nobody was sloppy, or too drunk to have fun in here, and so they talked DC versus Marvel, the new *Joker*, *Wonder Woman*, and *Supergirl*.

Then they went into the obscure ones, ones I had never even heard of before, even though someone brought up *Wolverine*, and I grinned. Yeah, Wolverine was my kind of guy.

My phone buzzed, and I pulled it out of my pocket.

Zoey: *Everything going okay?*

My heart sped up at the sight of her name, and I cursed. Shit, I couldn't get too close. Not when I didn't know what was happening. And, hell, not when we were just trying to figure out what was going on between us. We had to go slow, couldn't get too serious.

I almost didn't text her back, but then I didn't want to be an asshole either. There had to be a middle ground.

Me: *We're at the comic shop now.*

Zoey: *I love that you're doing that. Finding anything you like?*

Me: *I'm just watching them. Making sure they don't act like idiots.*

Zoey: *I'm glad that they have you. When are you done tonight?*

My dick pressed against my zipper, and I cursed at it. She wasn't asking me over, wasn't asking to see me. But, of course, my dick wanted her.

I ignored everything else inside me that wanted to see her, too. Because I had to ignore it. I couldn't be too needy.

Me: *We have that bar afterwards if they're still up for it, but I think John's getting tired. He's worked doubles all week, and I wouldn't blame him if he wanted to go home.*

Zoey: *I just left Lacey at home with a book so she could relax.*

I frowned, thinking I got the dates wrong.

Me: *She didn't stay out late for your bachelorette party?*

Zoey: *No, she didn't really want a big one. She already had that bridal shower. So, tonight, a few of us went out to dinner, but that was it. No huge stripper party or anything.*

Me: *Good. Because I really don't think you're allowed to go see strippers.*

Fuck, I hadn't meant to sound so possessive. Because I couldn't be that way with her. Zoey wasn't mine. We were just friends. Doing this casual thing.

Zoey: *Don't worry, mister. No strip clubs for me. I'm not a huge fan of glitter.*

Me: *Well, they would be wearing the glitter. And you better not get any glitter on you if you ever go to one.*

Zoey: *LOL.*

Me: *So, what are you doing now?*

Zoey: *Just hanging at home and reading. I should probably work on my accounting or do something. But I'm just not in the mood.*

Me: *You want me to stop over after I'm done?*

I hadn't actually meant to text that, but suddenly my fingers were moving, and I couldn't take it back.

Things were getting a little too serious, too fast, but I wanted to be near her.

Fuck.

Zoey: *If you want. It'd be nice to see you. It's been a couple of days. Unless you stay up too late with the boys.*

I looked up as John played with his phone, and the other guys started to slow down.

Me: *Give me an hour or two.*

Zoey: *See you soon.*

I ignored the way my gut clenched, and my heart raced at that.

Crap.

We couldn't be anything more than we were. I couldn't let that happen. But I had a feeling I was going to.

The guys and I ended up going to that bar, but only for about thirty minutes. They hadn't been in the mood, and frankly, I wanted to get out of there and get to Zoey. That probably made me a fool, but I couldn't help it. I was losing my mind when it came to her, and that thought just reminded me that I had already been losing my mind for many things.

I really should step away, but I knew I wouldn't.

I dropped John off at his place, and he just grinned over at me. "Thanks for tonight. I know it wasn't a rowdy night like most bachelor or stag parties, but I had fun."

I returned the smile.

"I had fun, too. Not every stag party needs to be a gorge of excess."

"Exactly. I'll talk to you soon, but thank you for everything. Seriously. I know I sort of dragged you into this, not quite kicking and screaming, but close enough."

"I didn't do anything I didn't want to do."

And that was the truth. I liked John, and I wanted to see him happy. And Lacey was the one who made him happy.

The fact that I was scarily falling for Lacey's sister was something I really didn't want to think about.

Because, fuck it. I wasn't allowed to fall for her.

"Have fun tonight, and say hi to Zoey for me." John winked as he got out of the car, and I froze.

"Huh?"

"I saw you texting tonight. Tell Zoey hi for me."

I cursed but shook my head, knowing I couldn't really deny it at that point. I wasn't going to lie to my friend, but I wasn't going to come out and say anything either.

I made sure John got inside and then pulled out of the driveway to head towards Zoey's house. I could stop right now. I could head home and say I was too tired. I could make sure to put distance between Zoey and me.

However, every time I thought of doing that, I couldn't. Because the reasons I was staying away were starting to sound a little thin the more times I said them. So, I just needed to trust myself and her not to fuck things up. But I couldn't get too serious. Not when I didn't know what my future held. Not when I was afraid that the next set of test results would come back not in my favor. If I ever got the damn results since my doctor was slow as fuck. My stomach hurt again, and it had nothing to do with the anticipation of Zoey. I promptly put those thoughts out of my mind and made my way to Zoey's door.

She answered as soon as I walked up, her grey jeans and soft top looking way too sexy on her. Her tousled blond hair lay over one shoulder, and it looked as if she had pulled it out of a braid. I hated that she looked so sexy, and I couldn't hold myself back from having thoughts of *more*. It was getting really hard to not want Zoey. Especially when I knew I needed to step away. But right then? I wasn't going to.

"So, you had fun?" Zoey said, stepping back so I could enter the house.

I leaned down and brushed my lips against hers, knowing it was a mistake as soon as I did it. She let out a surprised breath and then moaned as I deepened the kiss. Yes, I was going to hell. But I was going to enjoy every fucking minute of my time on the way there.

"Well, hello," she said, grinning, her eyes a little glassy.

"Hey, Zoey-girl. Yes, we had a good time. John is safe in his house and probably going to read one of the many comics he just bought."

"That's good. I know he doesn't have a lot of time to read these days."

"With his new job after the move, he's probably not going to have a lot of time for a while."

"Nope, but he has tonight. I'm glad that he didn't go crazy or anything and have too much fun."

"It's John, he wasn't ever going to go too crazy."

I followed her to the couch in the living room, and my dick hardened again, remembering what we had done on that sofa. She bit her lip, and I knew she was thinking about it, too.

Hell, my dick was already too hard, and I hadn't even really touched her.

"Did you enjoy your night?" I asked as we settled onto the couch. She leaned into me and nodded against my chest.

"We had fun tonight, too, but no one got too drunk. I didn't even drink at all, mostly because I don't like drinking out in public anymore. You know?"

My jaw tensed as I sat next to her on the couch, and she cuddled into me.

"Sorry, didn't mean to bring it up," she said quickly.

I shook my head, even though she couldn't see it.

You shouldn't be sorry for bringing it up," I growled out.

"I'm fine, though. Really." She pulled away even though I tightened my arms so she couldn't face me. "It was a long time ago, and you were there."

"You might be fine, but I still want to find that piece of shit and tear his arms off."

She smiled softly when I eased my grip, then leaned forward, her hand on my chest as she brushed her lips against mine. "Thank you."

"Don't fucking thank me for that."

"I meant thank you for still caring."

I sighed and then pulled her closer. "Want to watch another movie?"

She shook her head and then kissed me again. I groaned.

"Really?" I asked, my hands on her ass.

"Just not on this couch. I think I need to buy a bigger one if we're going to keep doing this." She smiled against my lips, and I was thankful that she didn't notice that I had stiffened. Because, Jesus, buying another couch? That sounded like a future. And, hell, I couldn't let her get too close.

So, instead, I kissed her harder and then maneuvered so I could stand and pick her up.

She let out a squeal and wrapped her legs around my waist. I made my way to her bedroom, her hands rubbing over my face as she stared at me.

Hell, I needed her, and it pained me to admit because I didn't want to need her just then.

So, I pushed those thoughts out of my head and

went back to kissing her. We were in the bedroom then, stripping each other of our clothes.

"I need you inside me," Zoey whispered, and my dick hardened even more. Impossible.

I pulled my shirt over my head, and she undid the belt on my pants, the sound of leather and the metal of the buckle making both of us groan. I lifted up her shirt and then undid her bra, her breasts falling heavily into my hands.

She let out a gasp as I pinched her nipple, and then I leaned down to suck the tip of it into my mouth. I wanted more. I wanted those little pink nipples to get all dark red and look like little cherries as I sucked and licked.

She moaned, pressing my head into her breasts, and I couldn't help but smile against her.

"Needy," I growled.

"Just like you," she said, and she wasn't wrong.

We undid my pants, and I stripped them off before I pulled her jeans down. And then we were naked, and I had my hands on her ass before I flipped her onto the bed.

"Ack!" she exclaimed, but I didn't pay attention. Instead, I went down to my knees and slid my mouth between her thighs.

She had one hand in my hair, the other gripping the edge of the bed as I licked and sucked and ate.

I parted her folds, looked down at her wet, glistening pussy, and kept licking. I hummed against her clit, loving the way she tightened her legs around my shoulders, and then I licked again, this time using two fingers to penetrate her. The inner walls of her pussy clamped around my digits, and I curled them, looking for the sweet bundle of nerves that I knew could make her go off in an instant.

Her body shook, and so did mine, my dick so hard I was afraid I would come right then, but I pressed that bundle, circled, and then pressed again, my thumb on her clit. She came hard, her pussy drenching my hand as she shook, calling out my name.

I kept going, pleasuring her again until she was right on the edge, and then stopped, pulling my fingers out and making sure her eyes were on mine as I licked my wet fingers one by one. Her eyes went dark, and her legs fell open, showing me every inch of her.

Her hands roamed up her chest, and she cupped her breasts. I quickly made a dash for the condom, sliding it over my length as I kept my eyes on her.

"Caleb," she whispered.

I nodded, unable to speak.

I positioned myself at her entrance and then pushed into her, one painstakingly slow inch at a time. She was so tight, and even after all the times we had been together since that first time, she was still tight. I had to close my eyes and try to think of England or baseball so I wouldn't come immediately. I wasn't even fully seated inside her yet.

Her hands clutched at my shoulders, so I leaned down to kiss her, and then I was deep inside her, both of us shaking as her inner walls clenched around my cock.

There were no words, there didn't need to be. I slid in and out of her, slowly at first, and then faster, harder. Until both of us were moving as one, on the brink of ecstasy. And then I moved my hand between us and played with her clit again so she would come with me.

"With me, Zoey-girl," I echoed my thoughts, and she nodded, clenching her inner walls.

My eyes crossed at that, and then I closed them, latching my lips to hers as she came hard, and I followed. I didn't shout her name, didn't do anything except kiss her. Because I was afraid. So afraid that, if I wasn't careful, I was going to fall.

And I couldn't, not when I was afraid that I didn't have the time I needed. Not when the unknown stared at me just like I stared into the abyss.

I kept my mouth on hers, and I kept moving, taking every ounce of pleasure that I could. Because this could be my moment, my present, and if I were lucky, maybe even my future. I didn't dwell on that, though, because I couldn't.

As we fell asleep together, her in my arms, I tried to

be okay. Attempted to think that I wasn't doing anything wrong. She didn't know that I was sick. Didn't know that we were still waiting on more brain scans.

And I knew that if I wasn't careful, I was going to break her heart. And possibly break mine, too.

Chapter 13

Zoey

SOMEHOW, TODAY WAS THE WEDDING REHEARSAL. IT seemed like only yesterday that I had walked into my mother's home, unknowing that everything would change so quickly. It honestly felt like a blink ago that my sister had handed me the tablet and the wedding book from hell, asking me to be her maid of honor.

I didn't regret doing this for my sister, though I did lament the amount of time it had taken.

However, I did get to know Caleb along the way, so maybe it was all worth it.

I shook my head. No, I wasn't allowed to think about him too often today. Even though he would be right there with me, for the entirety of the wedding rehearsal, and maybe a little bit after.

We didn't have plans that evening other than being near each other, and I couldn't help but want more.

How had I fallen for him so quickly?

I knew a crush from childhood and then on into adulthood was far different than what it was like to be with the man himself. And as I understood the different layers of him, and I got to feel him against me almost every night this week, I couldn't help but need.

It should've worried me, but it didn't. Not in the way that it probably should have.

I pushed thoughts of Caleb out of my mind because this was not about him. Today was all about Lacey and John. Okay, so the whole weekend was about them.

The wedding was on Saturday, and they'd scheduled the wedding rehearsal for Thursday. There had been another event booked for Friday at the place they were holding the rehearsal, so they'd made this work. Plus, John was able to make it work for his job, and now we were here at a beautiful, old, and rustic-looking farm, ready to have the rehearsal.

They would be getting married here on Saturday, as well, and I honestly could not imagine a better place for the two of them.

Because Lacey might seem chic and city-like, but she loved nature and adored old farmlands and mountains.

The same with John. Soon, they would be living in the big city and wouldn't have this view every day.

So, they were going to take advantage of every ounce of it that they could.

And I was happy that I could be a part of it.

The old farm was still a working farm, but they had made half of it a place for people to visit, and they had even built an inn on the grounds. We would be staying at the inn on Friday and Saturday night. Tonight, we'd be going home, which I didn't mind because I would probably need a break from Lacey and my family for a while.

Not that I didn't love them, but weddings always brought out the scary in people.

"Wow, pumpkin, you've sure done it, haven't you?" my dad asked, and I grinned and looked over at him.

"This was all Lacey."

He shook his head and wrapped his arm around my shoulder, kissing the top of my head. He had always done that, and it just reminded me of home.

Because when Mom and Lacey had been stuck at the hospital, Dad had been with me to make sure I got to school, help me with my homework, and to work far too many hours to make sure we could afford everything that my little sister needed.

It had never truly been him and me against the world, but he'd always been my person within the family.

"It looks wonderful. And I never would have thought

of having a wedding and a rehearsal at a farm. But this works."

"This doesn't really scream farm to me," I said honestly, looking around at the elegant area with the Rocky Mountain backdrop. He laughed.

And the place really didn't feel overly country. The inside of the old barn, the one that the farm owners didn't use anymore because they had built a refurbished one that was actually meant for farming, had been turned into a hall of sorts.

It was all grey wood and rustic-looking. There were long benches inside, as well as some outside since the weather had cooperated.

Everything had clean linens and white and light gold plates and accessories. The tables had been set beautifully, and I couldn't actually wait to see what would happen on the wedding day. The rehearsal was just part of it. This was but a glimpse into what the wedding day would be like, but the colors would be even more vibrant and stunning on Saturday.

"It looks beautiful, the lighting's great, and I know that your sister is going to have the time of her life, especially once she blinks and realizes that her future husband is standing at the other end of the aisle."

"She's been fun these past few weeks."

My dad laughed.

"That's a wonderful way of putting it, pumpkin." He

kissed the top of my head again and then gestured towards the man standing on the other side of the hall.

"And if my eyes aren't deceiving me, there's another man that I should probably be talking to. About you?"

I blinked and shook my head. "That's Caleb, Dad. You know Caleb."

He nodded. "I do. And I've seen the way you two look at each other. Should I get all big, bad dad on him?"

I froze but then laughed nervously. "Let's not. We're just, you know, friends."

"I don't want to know what that *'you know'* means. However, he makes you happy. I can see that. So that makes me happy. But just know that if he changes that somehow, I will kill him. I have my ways. It would be long and painful, and no one would miss him."

I actually didn't know if my dad was joking at that point. "You know, you should probably leave Caleb and go give this talk to John. After all, he's marrying your sweet baby girl."

"He's marrying *one* of my sweet baby girls." He squeezed my shoulder again, and then let go. "I should go and see where I'm supposed to be. If not, I'm sure Lacey will tell me." He rolled his eyes, and I laughed, shaking my head.

"Coast clear?" Caleb asked as he walked towards me.

"Were your ears burning?" I asked, laughing.

"Oh, not so much. More like every part of me because I saw the look your dad was giving me. He going to kill me?"

I shook my head and slid my arm around his waist. He held me close, and I did my best not to sigh like the Disney princesses that my friends tended to act like when they were thinking about their men.

I was *not* going to become them.

"He just wanted me to know that he would kill you for me if needed."

"That's nice."

From the way that he spoke, I didn't think that he thought that was nice at all. However, we didn't have time to focus on what that meant, or what we meant, because the wedding rehearsal was about to start.

I said goodbye to Caleb and then went to Lacey's side as she went through her notes and looked around.

"Okay, we'll get this done. Marni, are you doing okay, doll?"

We all looked over at John's sister, who currently sat on one of the chairs near us. She patted her very round belly.

"We're doing just fine here. Still have a couple of weeks until the due date. Don't worry."

Lacey smiled, but I didn't know if there was much glee in that grin. "Oh, I'm not worried. That baby will not be coming on Saturday." She knocked on wood, and I swore threw salt over her shoulder. Where she got the salt? I had no idea. "You'll be fine, and then, in a couple of weeks, we'll welcome a new member to the family. Everything in a nice, logical order."

I barely resisted the urge to look at my mother. Because I had a feeling my mom was probably praying right along with Lacey at that point.

A bridesmaid giving birth on or during the wedding probably wasn't a good omen for anyone. But Marni looked fine, and we still had time.

"Okay now, this is how it's going to go," Lacey began, but before she could get too far into her tirade, John came around and dipped her into a very deep, nearly inappropriate kiss.

That sent titters through Lacey, and I smiled, unable to help myself.

"Well, hi," Lacey said.

"Hey there. I just wanted to make sure you knew that I loved you. And I cannot wait for Saturday. Everything looks great, light and love of my life. This is going to be amazing, no matter what happens, because in the end, I'm going to be your husband and you're going to be my wife. And nothing else in the world matters except for that. So, take a breath, and know that I love you. Okay?"

Tears were freely flowing down my cheeks as well as

Lacey's at that point. My mother sniffled, and I swallowed hard as Caleb handed over a tissue.

"Thanks," I gasped, wiping my face. "Where did you get this?"

"Lacey made sure all of us had a pack of tissues in our pocket. We'll have some for the wedding, too."

I held back a laugh. Of course, Lacey did. She really did think of everything. And while I knew my maid of honor—if I ever got married—was going to be amazing and helpful, I had a feeling that Lacey was going to be right alongside her. However, I wasn't getting married anytime soon, and I purposely didn't look over at Caleb as I thought those things.

"Okay, let's get this rehearsal going. Caleb and Zoey? Get close. Because you guys are going to be attached at the hip for the rest of this wedding."

Caleb slid his arm around my waist again, and I sighed dramatically into him.

"On it," I said, and everyone laughed.

Lacey narrowed her eyes at us, but then went back to dictating the wedding.

Or planning it, whatever.

The rehearsal went quickly, and then it was time for the food. My favorite part.

There would be courses served and lovely cheese spreads and desserts and cake for the wedding. Tonight, though, was all about the pizza.

"Pizza and wine for a wedding rehearsal?" Caleb asked.

"Oh, this isn't delivery pizza. And it's not DiGiorno," I said, making Caleb laugh.

"Okay, tell me, what's so special about this?"

"Everything is cooked right in front of you in that wood-burning oven. You pick exactly what toppings you want. If you want to go classic with some Margherita pizza or pepperoni. Or if you want to go completely hipster and add some arugula and pears and whatever you want to it. You have fun, and the chef is sure to have the ingredients."

"I'm not putting arugula on my pizza," Caleb said dryly.

"I don't know, I've had it before. It's really good.

"Fine. You can put arugula, but if you touch my pizza with pineapple, we're going to have words."

I didn't tell him that I actually liked ham and pineapple pizza. I already had to hide it from so many, might as well hide it from Caleb, too.

Everybody got their own pizza, and I groaned as I bit into the whole wheat crust, the cheese melting and almost burning my mouth.

"This is amazing," I grumbled around my bite.

"Can't talk, dying in bliss."

I laughed and looked over at Caleb as he practically demolished his pizza. He hadn't been eating that much recently when we'd been near each other, and I figured work was hard, or he wasn't that hungry. I just didn't know.

And that kind of worried me.

We were going steadily into this almost serious relationship, and he hadn't really told me much about himself. I didn't know everything, and he was pretty closed-off. I had to remind myself that even though we had been friends forever, we hadn't been in this new part of our relationship for long.

I didn't have to know every single secret, I just wished he would open up a bit.

Then again, I was holding the worst secrets from him.

The fact that I had loved him as the Caleb of my dreams for as long as I could remember, and the fact that I was totally falling for him now.

He looked over at me and winked before taking a bite of mine. I knew I didn't have a plan when it came to making Caleb fall in love with me. And the thing was, I had done the exact opposite. I had fallen for him even more than before, and I had no idea how he felt about me.

I ignored that, ignored the Caleb of my dreams, and focused on the Caleb of my present.

Because I was so afraid that if I didn't, if I didn't live

in the moment, there wouldn't be a Caleb going forward.

As someone who tried her best to plan for anything, I didn't know what the next step was. Or how I should feel.

Or if I'd have a Caleb at all in any part of my future.

Chapter 14

Caleb

I GROANED, SLIDING MY HANDS OVER ZOEY'S THIGHS before I went back, licking, sucking. Her taste exploded on my mouth, and I shifted my hips, my dick so hard, I was surprised I could still see straight as I lapped at Zoey's pussy.

"I'm going to go if you don't slow down," I growled, and then went back to humming along her clit.

Zoey answered by sucking my cock deeper down her throat, swallowing so that I felt the suction along my length. My eyes practically crossed at the sensation that spread all over my body from that touch. I let out a breath, trying to focus on the delectable task at hand.

But it was really hard to do when my cock was in her mouth.

"You have to come first," she panted, and then went back to sucking.

I shook my head, even though I knew it was ridiculous because she couldn't see me with my head between her legs. However, it didn't matter. I wanted the taste of her in my mouth, and I was pretty sure I was going to blow if I wasn't careful.

So, in answer, I sucked on her clit, penetrated her with two fingers, thrust in and out of her as she clamped her thighs around my head. When she came, I continued my sucking and licking for a few moments before I moved so quickly, she couldn't reach out for me.

I sheathed myself in a condom and was inside her balls-deep before she could even let out another breath. I stayed still for a few seconds, trying to catch my breath as she squeezed around me, tight, slick, and all mine.

No, fuck, not all mine. It would be good to remember that fact.

"Dear. God." Her nails dug into my back, and I pounded into her, my body shaking, sweat-slick as I latched my mouth to hers. "I can taste myself," she muttered against my mouth, and I grinned.

"Sweet, and fucking *mine*," I muttered and kept going, thrusting deeper with each stroke, wanting her to climax again as I did.

She arched up, her breasts pressing into my chest as she wrapped her legs around my waist harder.

I thrust deep once more, and she came, her whole body shaking as her eyes went wide, her pupils dilated. Just the look of it, her mouth parted, her rapturous gaze only for me, I came right then, unable to hold back. I fell on my side, my cock still buried deep inside her as I ran my hands over her body, through her hair, wanting to touch her.

I just wanted to be with her. And that worried me.

This was getting far too serious, too quickly.

I knew that.

I knew I should be safe and not do something stupid like fall for her when I didn't know what was going on outside of us, but I couldn't help it. I was falling so hard and so fast that it scared the fuck out of me.

And I couldn't really do anything about it. Not then.

So, I just held her and kept my gaze on hers as she leaned into my strokes, smiling like a cat in cream.

"It's a wonderful way to wake up," she whispered, nibbling on my chin.

I leaned back so I could look at her again.

"You liked that?" I asked her.

"I loved it."

She looked at me then, and I swore my heart stopped.

Hearing the word *love* from her scared me. Not that I

was afraid of that emotion in general, but I didn't know what the fuck was going on with me. I wasn't a good bet. My head still hurt like hell. Yesterday, I'd called the doctor, demanding results. They said they were still waiting, and I hadn't even been able to talk to my physician. I hated my fucking doctor's office. They were worthless, and I knew I needed a second opinion.

However, I hadn't even gotten a real first opinion yet.

I was scared. I felt like I was always scared these days. "You're off today, right?" Zoey asked, and I nodded.

"Yes, but I have tons of errands to run and shit to deal with before the wedding."

I also had another doctor's appointment, but I didn't tell her that. I didn't know why. I pretty much told her everything else these days. My whole family knew about the migraines and the hallucination I'd had once and the fact that there were no clear test results at the moment, but I hadn't told *her*.

Did that make me a piece of shit? Probably. She needed to know what was going on with me, but I was afraid to say anything. And I didn't know why. Things were going far too fast for us in recent weeks, and I knew it.

I needed to find a way to slow things down. I just didn't know how. We saw each other almost every day because we had the same friends, and she was best friends with the women in the family. With Lacey's wedding the next day, I couldn't really avoid her.

And I hated that I'd just thought the word *avoid* when I didn't want to avoid her at all. That fact worried me most of all. Because I didn't have answers, and I felt like I actually needed them if I was going to continue this relationship with her.

I was such a fucking asshole, but I didn't know how to fix things.

I didn't know if there *was* any fixing it.

"I'm glad you're not working today, mostly because you know…the wedding and all."

I grinned. "I'm going to see if John needs me for most of the day. However, he's pretty steady, and he's spending some time with his family and Lacey before the big day."

"And I get to help with all of the little nitty-gritty details because Lacey has already texted me, I think four times." She leaned over me, her breasts right in my face as she looked for her phone. "Six. Six times."

I lapped at her nipple, sucking. She groaned, rocking against me, her pussy wet and pressing against my thigh.

She let out a shaky breath. "Okay, enough of that, we have to get going. I have to see what Lacey wants."

I hummed against her breasts and played with her ass, sliding my fingers between her crease.

"Caleb. We need to stop. We need to be responsible."

I nodded and let her breast go with a resounding pop.

She didn't really want me to let go, I could tell.

"You're right, even though I'd rather stay in bed. I've got things to do." Like a doctor's appointment I really didn't want to go to.

She grinned and looked down at me, her eyes filled with something I didn't want to name. Because I was too chickenshit. Because what if I really was sick? I didn't want to burden her with that. She deserved so much more than someone who had no idea what the fuck was going on.

Because the doctor still hadn't ruled out any neurological diseases, and I hadn't heard anything else. For something that apparently needed to be taken care of quickly, he hadn't done a single thing for me. I did not want to go to this doctor's appointment.

"What's wrong?" she asked, and I shook my head, grinning at her. I had to look like everything was fine. Because it was. Everything had to be fine, at least for her. She had enough stress with Lacey, I didn't want to add to that.

"Nothing. You should go get ready."

"I know. I'll see you at the wedding, though?"

"I'm the best man. Got to be there."

She grinned, then she kissed me again and hopped out of bed.

We hadn't actually discussed if we were each other's dates, and I was glad for that. Because things were getting so serious, I needed to settle down. I just didn't know how. She packed up her bag and headed out just as I was getting into the shower.

"Have a good day. Don't work too hard." She frowned and leaned over to rub at my temple.

"You look like you have a headache. Are you doing okay?" she asked.

I smiled, trying to look like I was just fine. I wasn't. "I'm doing good. Stop worrying about me. I'm a grown man."

She looked down at me, wearing nothing but my skin, and grinned. "Yeah, I know you're a grown man."

I would've blushed, but I was used to this. Zoey was sweet, tempting, and yet could probably outdo me with dirty jokes.

And I wasn't ready for her. Had never been. Even when I'd only thought of her as a friend, I'd never been ready for what Zoey could give me.

I needed to slow things down. Needed to figure out exactly how to get that done.

"Go," I growled, and she smiled and then hopped right out, her bag in hand.

We didn't keep anything at each other's homes. We didn't think we were there yet, or maybe we were, and she sensed that I wasn't ready. We hadn't called each other boyfriend or girlfriend or added any other labels. Which was good. I sure as hell didn't want them.

I needed to figure out my own shit, and then maybe I could figure out Zoey.

Hell, I just didn't know. We'd been together in some fashion for what? Months at this point. Jesus Christ. How had that even happened? It had been almost a full season already, and we were doing really good about not putting any form of label on what we had.

I was a jerk. I wasn't treating her right. I knew that. Only I was still waiting to figure out what the fuck was wrong with me. Endless tests had come up with nothing. And I felt like I couldn't make any other decisions until I knew what was going on. Maybe it was stupid. Maybe it was just a roadblock in my mind, but it was my mind, the decision I had already made. So, I was going to stick with it. After I'd jumped into the shower, trying to make it quick, my head started to pound.

I staggered out of the stall and to the toilet and threw up everything in my stomach. It wasn't much since I hadn't even had coffee yet. I sat there, pulling a towel under me and drip-dried as I tried to breathe.

Jesus. If that wasn't an omen, I didn't know what was.

I tried to get my head to stop pounding for a little bit longer, and then I grabbed my phone to text Devin. My eyes hurt, and I narrowed them, hoping I was texting well enough that the words would make sense, at least with autocorrect.

Me: *Can you drive me to my doctor's appointment?*

Devin: *When is it?*

Me: *In about an hour.*

Devin: *I'm on my way. Need anything?*

I needed answers. I needed to know what the fuck to do about the woman that I was falling for. The one I shouldn't fall for. I needed so many damn things that weren't available right now that I knew I was probably going to mess everything up as soon as I took the next step.

Instead, I told Devin no and got dressed as quickly as I could. I was just grabbing my wallet and keys when Devin unlocked the door and walked in without even knocking.

"Good, you're standing."

"I'm glad that you didn't bother to knock," I said, trying to smile. My right eye was pulsating, and I was having trouble seeing.

Great, another fucking migraine.

"Seeing as the three of you rarely use the doorbell before you just walk into my house, I don't feel bad. Plus, I was worried. Sue me."

"I'm not angry. I'm glad you came in. The sound of the doorbell or a knock may actually set me on edge." I put on my sunglasses even though I was inside, the light starting to hurt my eyes.

"Another migraine?" Devin asked, his voice low.

"No surprise there. But, hell, at least my doctor, if I ever actually get to see the man, will see me in a full-blown migraine."

"What do you mean?"

"I rarely see him. He shows up for like two minutes to prescribe some tests, but I'm always with the nurses or the PA. I'm not actually with the doctor, who's supposed to diagnose me." I didn't know if that was how it was supposed to be done. I had been healthy for all of my life, so having to actually see a doctor who wasn't just a general practitioner was new for me. I was out of my depth here, and I felt like I was drowning.

"I fucking hate our healthcare system." Devin shook his head.

"Don't even get me started."

"It sucks ass. I know Tucker is dealing with a bunch of things with Evan, too."

"Hell, how is Evan?" Tucker's son was in remission thanks to a bone marrow transplant as well as every other procedure the kid had been put through, but things were still scary.

"Doing okay, but there was an insurance issue, so Evan is stuck in the hospital overnight rather than getting sent home because he won't be able to get the right meds unless he's in the hospital. Tucker's staying with him while the parents get some sleep. But I think they're all exhausted at this point."

"Jesus. I thought Evan was doing better."

"He is, but he still needs meds, and if his doctors don't order the right scripts, and if the insurance doesn't cover them like it should, things get stirred up."

"I know. Hence why I really need your help today."

"Well, I'm here for you." He paused, frowning. "Though I'm actually wondering why you didn't ask Zoey."

I looked down at my feet before we made our way out.

"Are you kidding me? You haven't fucking told her that you're sick?"

"I didn't want to worry her. She has so much to do with the wedding and shit."

"No, that's just a cop-out. Why the hell are you scared to tell her that you're sick?"

I let out a sigh, not knowing what the right answer was since I didn't even have one for myself. "I don't know. Maybe because I need to figure this out on my own first. I wasn't expecting Zoey. We're just casual. You know? Nothing serious."

"Are you telling me that or yourself?"

"Fuck you." I already hated myself enough, and

probably would even more by the time things were over. I didn't need Devin on my ass about it, too.

"No, fuck you if you hurt her."

"Come on, let's go to the doctor," I grumbled.

"What are you going to do about Zoey?" Devin asked.

"I don't know. I think it's time to cool things off, though, you know?"

"No, I really don't."

"I don't want anything serious. Especially when I'm trying to figure things out with myself. With the wedding and everything, things just got too deep, too quick."

"You fucking hurt her, you're going to have to deal with us."

"I thought you were my brother, not hers."

"I *am* your brother, and that's why I'll kick your ass once you're healthier. Because I love you, you dumb shit. Don't do anything stupid."

I pulled up my phone and looked down at it, knowing I was going to be even dumber in a moment. I could tell her, but I didn't want her to worry. I didn't want her to look at me like I was different. I had known deep down that she had always had a little thing for me, even if it was a little crush. If she looked at me differently, I wouldn't be able to stand it. Because I didn't want to be different. I wanted to be fine. But I wasn't going to be okay if I didn't find the answers. And that meant I needed some space from Zoey. Even if it was the worst possible time. And to do that, I needed to make sure that she had an easy way out.

I knew exactly what I needed to do to make sure she got her space.

Me: *Hey, what are you doing tomorrow?*

Christy: *I was planning on cleaning my house. Why? You have something better in mind?*

Me: *What do you say about going with me to a wedding?*

As I waited for her answer, my stomach roiled, and I wanted to throw up again. But this time, it had nothing to do with the migraine.

Chapter 15

Zoey

"Before I do this wedding thing, I have a couple of things to say to you," Lacey said, and I froze, my back going ramrod straight.

I really was a little afraid of exactly what Lacey was going to say. My entire life had been centered around Lacey and this wedding for the past couple of months. And the fact that I kept saying the mantra of *I love my baby sister* over and over in my head just to remind myself of that fact spoke volumes.

Lacey wore a beautiful white lace and silk robe, her hair already done in long, blond curls, the extensions she had put in last month perfect for the half-Elsa braid that she wanted.

She looked gorgeous, like a perfect bride, and while I wasn't jealous, I was a little worried about what was going to happen next. Not that I thought John was going to leave her at the altar or anything, mostly because Lacey had become more and more intolerable over the past couple of days, and I was exhausted.

I really didn't want to deal with any last-minute scary issues when it came to this wedding.

"Okay?"

Lacey winced and reached out, gripping my hands with hers, her nails perfectly manicured. I had a similar manicure done, but I had already messed up one nail, and my hands were full of cuts, and a little set of scars and gouges.

However, the flowers for this wedding looked phenomenal.

If I did say so myself.

"The fact that you just looked at me with apprehension tells me I truly have been the world's worst bride."

I shook my head. "No, you haven't. I'm sorry if I made you feel that way."

"No, you don't apologize to me. I know I leaned on you a lot for this wedding. I know it's been hard, and I've been a beast. I love you, and I wanted to thank you for being amazing throughout this whole experience. I know you didn't really sign up for this, and I kind of threw you to the wolves. The wolves being me. And possibly Mom."

We both smiled, but thankfully, Mom wasn't in the room to hear the comment.

"Lacey—" I began.

My sister held up her hand, her teeth worrying her lip for a moment before she seemed to realize that her makeup was already done and stopped. "No, let me finish, I promise I'll be quick. I love you so much. I wanted this day to be perfect, and I know I was over-bearing. I know I made it all about me, and John, but mostly about me."

I didn't refute that comment, but it was a bride's prerogative, and I didn't blame her for that. Plus, I knew John didn't mind at all.

"Throughout it all, you were always there for me, but I feel like I was cruel to you. I forced you to work on my timetable and do far more than any other maid of honor would do. I should've hired an actual wedding planner, that way, you could focus on just the flowers and being my sister. And maybe on a potential amazing romance with a certain best man." She winked, and my face flamed.

"Lacey."

"What? I was rude to you. I was a bitch. Let's be honest."

"Well…" I trailed off, and she rolled her eyes.

"I really was a horrible person. It's because I suck at this whole communication thing and getting things in the right order. I had my reasons, and you know them. But those reasons don't negate the fact that I was cruel. I never want to be that person again. I know we're only a couple of hours or less away from the wedding ceremony, from walking down that aisle and seeing John and I don't want to have those bad feelings on my mind because of the way I treated you."

"Today is supposed to be about you. Always."

"Perhaps, and you're right, but I still didn't need to be mean to you. And I didn't need to be callous when it came to your relationship with Caleb. Or the fact that I didn't even allow you to talk about it with me at all. I know you have your girlfriends, and I know you've probably talked with them, considering Caleb's part of that group, as well. Only I haven't even said a damn thing about the two of you, other than the one time where I was a harpy. I'm so happy for you. I know he is that shining star for you. He's your John. I've always known."

I blushed, ducking my head. "Lacey, we're still new."

And I love him. But I wasn't going to say that out loud.

"You've had a crush on him since we were little."

My head shot up. "You're not supposed to mention that."

"And I'll never tell him. I swear. But the fact that you guys are together? It's like fate."

"We haven't talked about it yet. We're not there." I tried to reiterate it, even as my heart sped up, and I warmed inside at the thought of him.

"I just wanted to make sure that you know that I'm so happy for you. And, yes, today is all about me and John and our romance, but I'm glad that there'll be another romance there. Because I want to watch you and Caleb dance tonight, for your first dance at a wedding."

"We're seriously not on that path. I don't know what path we're on, but we're taking things slow."

"John and I took things slow, and it worked out. Just know that I'm so happy for you. And Caleb is a great guy. And I can't wait to see what happens."

"I love you, Lacey. Even if you're really unbearable." I mumbled the last part, and she laughed. I held her close and blinked back tears.

"I can't cry," she said. "Even though I have the best makeup on, that is supposed to be able to withstand hurricane tears, I don't want to chance it."

"Same." I closed my eyes and hugged her tightly. She was so strong, even with her slightly frail body. There was power within those bones, even if they tried to take her from me long ago. Strength within that soul. And she might have lost her way a bit, but we were allowed to do that sometimes. And I didn't mind. Because she was my baby sister. And she was getting married.

I did my best to push thoughts of Caleb from my mind, only because tonight wasn't about us. I didn't want to put too much into it, to rely on what we could be too heavily.

Because even though we were together, even though I knew there was something there, he was very good at putting distance between us. So, I wasn't going to let myself be hurt. I was going to let myself love him, but I was also going to let time pass. Because that's what we needed. Time. To just be with each other.

"Okay, girls, it's time to get dressed," my mother announced as she walked into the room, and I smiled.

"Wedding time!" I said, and Lacey did a little booty shake before we all went to the staging area.

We helped Lacey into her dress, and we wiped at tears, grateful that our makeup was the way it was, and the makeup artist was there to help with any streaks that might have dared roll down our faces.

I quickly put on my dress, grateful for the champagne gold that made me feel like a princess. We would match the romance of fall ambiance perfectly. I loved my dress and would possibly wear it again if I ever had a gala or something to go to. Maybe Caleb would have one, and he would take me.

I grinned, sliding my hands down my soft dress, imagining Caleb.

I really needed to stop.

We hadn't even discussed our feelings, we'd been really good about focusing on everyone else and living in the moment, and I needed to be better at that.

"Um, Zoey?" Marni, John's very pregnant sister, said from my side.

I looked over at her as she rubbed her back, and my eyes widened.

"Please tell me you just have a backache."

"How much longer until the wedding?" she asked, her voice a little breathy.

"Soon. Are you in labor?" I whispered fiercely, making my voice so low, I hoped no one could hear.

"Possibly. My water hasn't broken yet, and this isn't my first go-around. I should be fine during the ceremony itself, but if we can make it quick, that would be amazing."

"Sounds perfect," I bit out, trying to be quiet. "Everything is fine."

"Everything is fine," she repeated.

We looked at each other, and I really hoped to hell everything was going to be fine.

"What's wrong?" my mother asked, looking between us.

"Um, nothing?" I lied.

"You're in labor, aren't you," my mother said, and I winced.

"I'm sorry, ma'am. I didn't mean to." Marni blushed.

"They are babies, you can't control when they show up. Are you okay?"

"I'll be fine for a little bit. It just started, but I know what labor feels like."

"What's wrong?" Lacey asked, coming up between us, her eyes wide, looking gorgeous in her long, white dress with lace and a princess train.

"Nothing," all three of us said at the same time.

"Oh my God, you're in labor," Lacey said, her hands shaking. "Okay. This is fine. Do we need to take you to the hospital? I can drive you right now."

I blinked at her, then looked at Marni, who looked just as confused.

"Lacey, it's your wedding. You can't drive her." I tried to be patient, but she just glared.

"The hell I can't. That's my niece or nephew in there, and if they need me to drive them to the hospital right now, I will. Screw my wedding."

"My God, hell's frozen over," I said, and my mother elbowed me in the side.

Marni smiled, however, looking strong and beautiful. "I'm really okay, Lacey. We're just going to make it through the ceremony, and then I'm going to head over to the hospital."

Lacey looked down at my mother's diamond watch

and nodded tightly. "Okay, then. We're going to make this quick. Come on, let's go marry the love of my life so we can go get a baby."

She picked up her dress and started stomping towards the door, and I just couldn't hold back my laughter any longer.

"Who are you?" I asked.

She looked over her shoulder and winked. "Not a bitch. That's not who I am anymore. But, seriously, let's get this thing done. I want my husband, and that baby isn't going to wait long for us."

I laughed and followed her and ran smack into Caleb as I walked out the door. "Hey, did you hear?" I said, running my hands down his very sexy suit. He had on a gold pocket square that matched my dress, and I just wanted to fix it for him and keep running my hands down him.

He looked at me then, his eyes serious, a frown on his face. "I did, she okay?"

"She's going to be fine. But we may have to be a little quick with the vows." I winked as I said it and tried to search his face for something. But I saw nothing. He was so closed-off. It worried me.

"What's wrong, Caleb?"

"Nothing. But I just wanted to let you know that I might not be staying that long after the ceremony and first part of the reception when I'm needed. My date Christy and I have plans."

I froze, blinking. I had clearly heard wrong. "What?"

Ice slid over me, and I felt like I was watching from the outside. I couldn't breathe, couldn't take it. A date? He had a *date*?

"Yeah." He cleared his throat. "Just friends. We're not romantic or anything. I wouldn't do that to you. But I figured, you know, since wedding dates and all were a step that we weren't ready to take, I made sure that I brought a friend. She's never really been to a wedding before. You know?"

He was rambling, and he didn't make any sense.

A date. He had brought a date. To my sister's wedding. The same wedding I was going to have to touch him and hold his arm as we walked up the aisle together towards photos and dinner and everything that came with a wedding.

I couldn't actually believe what he was saying.

When had things changed? I had let him inside me the day before, holding him as we made love. But, apparently, that had only been on my end. It had been sex for him. A quick fuck in the morning and then a *see you later*.

I knew that we had said we would just be friends who casually saw each other and saw where things went. But bringing a date to the wedding without even consulting me?

I had no words. Literally no words.

I just looked at him, my eyes dry—thankfully—and shook my head. "I need to go see my sister. You need to go get in position for the wedding." I knew my voice sounded wooden, but I didn't really have anything else to say.

He had brought a date, and I loved him.

I loved him, and I felt like I was breaking inside.

My mother gave me a sharp look as I smiled too brightly and blinked away any tears that might come.

"What's wrong?" she whispered.

"Nothing. Just really excited about the wedding and the baby coming. All big things all at once."

And my broken heart lay shattered between us, its shards icy as it stabbed into my feet when I took the few steps towards the wedding party.

"Baby, what's wrong?"

I shook my head. "Nothing. Nothing can be wrong right now. This day is for Lacey. We'll talk later."

"Okay. I love you."

Tears stung my eyes, and I nodded. "I know. I love you, too."

"Okay, are you ready?" Lacey asked, and I nodded, averting my gaze so she wouldn't see the pain in my eyes.

I didn't want anyone to see. And yet I was going to be on display, a spectacle, I was going to have to show the world that I was fine, even though I was nothing of the sort. I was broken, dying, and there was nothing left for me.

The wedding began, and the very pregnant sister began her walk, breathing very quietly, even though I knew she had to be in pain. Her husband met her at the end, kissed her, and then her belly, to the cheers and sighs of nearly everyone in the room, and then went with her to sit at the bride's side, rather than standing. And then John's other two sisters went, and I followed, walking alone down my path towards the altar, keeping my gaze from my family. And Caleb.

I didn't look at him, I couldn't.

I just stood there, wondering what I was going to do.

Wondering what was left.

There was nothing left. There could *be* nothing left.

The wedding continued, and I didn't pay attention to any of it. I held my sister's bouquet when she handed it to me, and then I gave it back when that time came. I looked down at the flowers I had painstakingly worked on for hours, and I felt nothing. No joy, no pain. Nothing.

And then they announced Lacey and John as husband and wife, and John dipped my sister in the most romantic kiss I'd ever seen, one that sent tears to my eyes, and I was grateful that others were crying.

They would think that I was crying for the happiness of it all, not for the jagged remnants of who I once was.

And then the happy couple walked down the aisle, and Caleb took a few steps towards me, his hand out.

"Are you ready?"

I looked at him, the love of my life, the crush I'd had since I was little, and I smiled brightly, knowing I was showing teeth. "Of course," I said, my voice hoarse.

I slid my hand into his, and we walked calmly down the aisle. I ignored him. I ignored everyone.

As soon as we were around the corner where no one could see, I let go, and I kept walking, needing to breathe.

Photos would have to wait. I couldn't focus, I had to suck in a breath.

Was this a panic attack?

I didn't know. My chest hurt, and I tried to breathe, but I couldn't draw in air.

"Zoey."

I turned on Caleb, thankful that we were alone on this side of the barn.

But people could come by at any minute, and I couldn't focus.

"You need to go."

"Let's talk about this."

"No, you don't get to do this. This is my sister's wedding. And you're ruining this for her."

You're ruining everything for me.

He took a step forward, and I slammed my bouquet

into him, one hit after another, slam after slam, flowers and petals falling to the ground.

My hours of work were *nothing* as I looked down at what was my hope, my dreams, the way that I took care of myself, and it was nothing.

"She's just a friend. It's not what you think. I didn't want the two of us, you and me, to make a mistake, you know?"

I could hear the lies in his tone, and I didn't really care. I didn't know what the truth was anymore. I looked at him then, the tears falling freely down my face. I hated the fact that he'd made me cry.

"You know, you were allowed to break it off. You were allowed to call it casual. But you were never allowed to be mean. That's not you, Caleb. You were never mean."

He looked at me then and didn't say anything. Instead, he rubbed his temple and looked like he was hurting. I wanted to feel like it was okay that he was hurting. Because *I* was hurting.

"Zoey, it's not like that."

"I don't know what it is. Because I cannot believe you did that. And what hurts the worst? I think I hate you. I hate you so much right now." I let out a rough chuckle, but he didn't say anything. "You know what's even worse than that? I hate the way you make me feel.

The fact that I love you, and there's nothing I can do about it."

And as I bared myself to him, my heart shattered into a million pieces all around us, and I walked away towards the rest of the wedding party.

I would take the rest of the photos, even if I didn't have a bouquet, I would be the best sister I could be, and then I'd lay in shattered remains and wonder what the hell I had been thinking.

Because having a crush on Caleb Carr was one thing. Knowing that love could be unrequited was another.

Having that love thrown in my face in the worst way possible?

That wasn't something I'd ever prepared myself for.

Chapter 16

Caleb

I DIDN'T GLOWER, I DIDN'T SCOWL. I DIDN'T FUCKING smile. I was such a loser. I had known the minute I texted Christy to see if she wanted to come with me to the wedding as a show of support rather than an actual date that it had been a mistake. But I hadn't been able to think of anything else to do.

Could I have actually talked to Zoey? Sure. But I didn't have my head on straight, and that was fucking clear.

So, now, I stood for the wedding photos, standing by John as the other man looked at me, knowing something was wrong, but he wasn't going to ask.

And I wasn't going to fucking answer, either. Because I was not going to ruin this for my friend.

John and Lacey deserved for this day to be fucking perfect. And that meant I needed to leave soon.

The wedding had been beautiful, not that I'd really noticed because I'd been trying not to look at Zoey, who looked as if I had broken part of her.

And, fuck, I had.

She loved me. Jesus Christ.

She couldn't love me. I was such an idiot. I didn't deserve anything she gave me. I deserved to go to hell, to get my ass beat, and be left for dead. I knew I would hurt her, but I hadn't known it would be like this.

I hadn't known she would hate me.

Or maybe that's exactly what I wanted.

Because if she hated me, I wouldn't have to make a fucking decision. In the past, I'd always been the man who treated women like royalty, even if I never stayed, but that wasn't me right then.

No, not even a little bit.

Damn it.

"You doing okay?" one of the groomsmen asked. I nodded, smiling brightly, even though I knew it didn't reach my fucking eyes.

"Yeah, long day. But good wedding."

"So, you came here with Zoey, right?" the guy asked.

I shook my head. "No, I didn't." Because I made mistakes and couldn't fix them.

The guy's brows lifted. "Oh, so you're not with her?"

That was the question for the ages. But considering what I had done and what she'd said, I knew the answer now. And though it had been my goal, the taste of regret was bitter on my tongue.

"No, I'm not."

"So, you wouldn't mind if I asked her to dance?"

I had my hands on the guy's lapels before I even thought about it, and then Dimitri was on me, pulling mc back.

"Caleb. What the fuck?"

The groomsman sputtered. "Sorry, man. He said she was single, but guess I was wrong. I meant nothing. You and Zoey, you guys are great. I'm just going to go. Sorry about that."

"You going to tell me what the fuck that was about?" Dimitri asked as he tugged me towards the other end of the barn. There was no one around, and we were outside so no one could hear us, but hell, I just wanted to go fucking home. My head hurt, I needed to throw up again, and I was still waiting on my damn doctor to give me the damn results.

"I'm fine."

"Don't lie to me. That's one thing we don't do. We

don't lie. Mom and Dad lied enough for both of us. You know that."

"Don't. Don't bring up our sad parents and their sad drinking." That wasn't a conversation I really needed, and hell, we were all mentally healthier now. Devin getting with Erin had forced us all to look into our pasts, so that part of us wasn't hurting anymore.

"I'm not going to. I don't need to. Because I thought we had moved past that. Now, you going to tell me why you almost beat the shit out of that man because he thought Zoey wasn't yours? I was pretty sure she was."

"I don't want to talk about it."

Tucker and Devin came over soon after, both glowering at me.

"What the hell is going on? Family fight?" Tucker asked, frowning.

Dimitri snarled. "No, he almost beat the shit out of a groomsman for daring to talk about Zoey. But I don't really see Zoey around, so why don't you tell us what happened?"

"Nothing happened."

"Caleb?"

I closed my eyes and wished for death. Because, seriously. This was par for the course on this fucking day.

"Christy," I said, turning to her.

I noticed my brothers and Tucker glare at each other,

and then look directly at me. Their eyes felt like daggers digging into my back, but I ignored them.

"Hey, sorry for leaving you like that." I cleared my throat.

Christy smiled but it didn't look happy, more resigned. "Don't be sorry. The wedding's beautiful. But, hey, I know you said you had a girl, and I was here to help you make a decision. You were very clear about that. I'm going to go."

"Jesus Christ," Dimitri grumbled.

"I'm going to fucking kick your ass," Devin grumbled.

"Not if Amelia does it first," Tucker whispered.

"I'm sorry," I said, ignoring them. "I'm an asshole."

"You are," Christy said, raising her chin. "Not to me, though. You were clear and upfront regarding what this was about. And I only said yes because I wanted to make sure that you knew you had fallen. I came here as your friend, not to hurt anyone. But I clearly think I did. So, you *are* the asshole. But not to me," she said again. "You better fix this, Caleb. Fix it quick, or you're going to lose the best thing you ever had."

And then she walked off, and I just shook my head. Hell, Christy was right, but I couldn't fix this. I didn't even know if there *was* anything to fix at this point.

"Okay, you're going to tell me what happened right

now, or I'm going to fucking kick your ass," Dimitri said, his muscles bulging beneath his jacket.

"And be quick about it," Devin mumbled.

"I'm fine," I lied.

"You may be fine, but Zoey clearly isn't," Tucker said, practically spitting the words.

"I knew something was off during the wedding, but I didn't think you had actually brought a fucking date to Zoey's sister's wedding," Dimitri snapped. "I thought I raised you better than that."

I flipped him off. "You didn't raise me."

"Okay, that's enough," Devin said, sliding between us. "You don't get to do this. You don't get to lash out because you're hurting. Is it because of the doctor? That can't be it."

I looked away, shame crawling over my skin.

"You still didn't fucking tell her," Devin said. "Are you serious?"

"I don't know what to say. You know the doctor didn't have anything to say, he didn't even show up. Just the nurse saying they were still waiting on more test results, and they would probably give me more details later. But they all sounded worried. You were there."

Devin nodded. "Yeah, I was there. They were worried because they didn't have answers, not because they thought that you were going to die."

I flinched, taking a step back. "Don't say things like that."

"Why? It's clearly running through your head. That's why you're being a dick to me and to everyone else. That's why you pretty much broke Zoey's heart. And don't lie and say you didn't. I know you did."

"I don't have anything to say," I said, taking a step back. My vision started to double, and bile filled my throat. My head pulsated, and I bent over, throwing up.

"Oh, fuck," Tucker said, and everyone started to move at once.

My body shook, and I dropped to my knees, my head pounding.

It hadn't come on this fast before. I couldn't breathe, couldn't focus.

The last thought I had was about Zoey, and I hated that I was going to ruin her sister's wedding. Just like I ruined everything else.

I WOKE UP SOON AFTER, but they still called an ambulance for me.

Thankfully, though, we hadn't disrupted the wedding since my brothers had been smart and called for the ambulance a little down the road. They'd dragged me that way since I hadn't been able to walk. Nobody from the wedding really knew what had happened. They were still partying and carrying on, at least that's what Dimitri said as he texted his wife.

I was grateful for that because I'd already ruined the day for Zoey, I didn't want to do it for everybody else.

We ended up in the emergency room, and they hooked me up to an IV for fluids, even though I really just wanted to go home. They took tests, and I waited. And kept waiting. All I wanted to do was throw up again.

"When's the last time you ate?" one of the nurses asked.

I frowned. "I don't know, yesterday or something? My head's been hurting."

"You're dehydrated, and your blood sugar's really low. I know it sucks to eat when you have a migraine, but you need to take care of yourself. Don't worry, we'll get you some fluids and some nutrients. The doctor will be here soon to talk to you about everything. We'll get you settled."

She checked all of my vitals and then walked out, leaving me alone in my little ER room with my brothers and sister. Tucker paced outside in the waiting room, apparently having wanted to allow the Carrs privacy. Thea and Erin were also in the waiting room, Thea with her feet up since the pregnancy made her feet swell.

Apparently, one of the bridesmaids, Marni, John's

sister, was also here in the hospital, only she was in the maternity ward.

It was a big day for hospital visits.

Hell.

"Why didn't you eat?" Dimitri asked, not looking at me as he spoke.

"I felt like crap. I didn't mean to forget."

"You need to take better care of yourself," Amelia said, her hands folded over her stomach.

Devin wrapped his arm around her shoulders and kissed the top of her head. "We all need to make sure we watch out for each other. This doesn't get to happen again."

"Well, what if it does? What if it's a neurological disease or a tumor they couldn't find in the first tests? We've been waiting how long? And I still don't have any answers."

"Then we'll do this together."

I looked at my sister as she spoke and sighed. "I've been doing just fine on my own," I mumbled.

"That's bullshit," Dimitri said. I turned my gaze towards him. "Complete bullshit. You came to us, you asked for help, and now you're pushing us away? I get that you're hurting, and you fucked up with Zoey, but you're going to have to find a way to make this right. We're going to find out whatever the fuck is wrong with you and make it better. Because Carrs don't back down. And you don't get to be sick anymore."

If I didn't feel like shit, I would have smiled just then. Dimitri would find a way to fix everything, even if some things weren't fixable. I leaned back against the pillow and let them mumble to each other as I tried to focus.

Making sure things didn't get serious with Zoey had been a mistake.

I had known that even as I was doing it, but I couldn't go back now. And I didn't deserve her forgiveness if I ever got a chance to say that I was sorry. I would just have to live with my regrets, even if I didn't know what was going to come next.

"Mr. Carr?" an unfamiliar voice said, and I opened my eyes to see a doctor in a white coat, a frown on his face.

"That's me," I said, my voice growly.

"We're his family," Dimitri said, ever the eldest brother.

"Well, I have a few things to go over with you if you don't mind. Do you want them out?"

I shook my head and then winced.

"I wouldn't shake your head with a migraine. You know that. So, I have your permission to go over some results with you in front of your family?"

"Yes. They get to know everything."

"Okay, then." The doctor took a seat next to me, and

I looked into his grey eyes, took in his greying hair, and I felt more at peace than I ever had with the other asshole I'd been talking with.

"First up, Dr. Johnson is no longer at this hospital. We've removed all his privileges. From now on, I will be working with your case."

I sat up quickly and then almost threw up.

"Stop moving so fast," the doctor said. "I'm Dr. Martinez. I will be helping you out."

"What the fuck do you mean about Dr. Johnson?" Dimitri said. And then he whispered, "Sorry about the cursing."

"No problem. You're probably going to be cursing a little bit more soon. Dr. Johnson no longer has privileges here, like I said. He hasn't been able to determine what tests to order, and now that we've been going over things with him, I wasn't happy with his work. So, I'm taking over, and we're going to get you fixed."

I sat there, blinking, a cold sweat sliding over me.

"You let him work with people for a year, and he's been *wrong*?" I asked, flabbergasted.

"No," Dr. Martinez said, a little growl in his tone. I didn't think it was about me, more about the fact that Dr. Johnson had fucked up. "I can't go into much of it. Suffice it to say, he didn't do a poor job with everyone. But he did miss a few things and failed to order some of the correct testing for others."

"What are you saying?"

"I'm saying I looked over the tests he gave you, and I can give you a diagnosis."

I swallowed hard, my body shaking. A real diagnosis. My God.

Dr. Martinez continued. "You have severe cluster headaches and migraines that could possibly cause hallucinations. You've only had the one, according to your chart. That could have been due to the environment, we won't rule anything out as of yet. We're going to monitor you, but you're going to be fine. It's not a tumor, it's not a neurological disease. Dr. Johnson should've been able to tell this from the tests he ordered, but perhaps he hadn't seen this exact illness before. I'm not sure. But I'm here to help you. You will be fine. I'm going to be with you for the entire process. My team is great, and we're going to call in some specialists, too, just to double-check that we're on the right path. You'll likely want a second opinion, and we're going to figure things out. Medicine is a science, but it also takes a lot of knowledge to work out the problem and put all the pieces together. So, we're going to get you on some migraine medication, both preventative and something for acute relief. And then we're going to figure out a long-term treatment plan for you. You are going to have a healthy and fulfilling life, and we're going to help make that happen."

I sat there and listened as the doctor talked with my

brother and sister about doctors, and treatments, and whatever else was going on. I didn't care. I just wanted that old doctor out of my life. I didn't really care what happened with the hospital.

Because, hell, I wasn't going to die. It wasn't a tumor or something that would take my faculties or anything. I had seriously been scared that this was the end. That I wouldn't be able to control things anymore, that this was it.

I had fucked everything up with Zoey because I hadn't had the right test results, and I was scared. And I had been too chickenshit to do anything about my fears.

The doctor went over a few things about my treatments and set up a whole battery of new tests and appointments so we could start on a fresh page.

I had meds waiting for me. I still couldn't quite believe it was this easy.

All I'd needed was a doctor who cared, one who could actually read a test result. It was no wonder I had always hated the healthcare system.

Because it had fucked me over, and then I had fucked myself over again.

Afterward, my family left me alone, mostly because I was like a bear with a thorn in my paw. I couldn't breathe, couldn't think.

Because I didn't know how to fix this. Not myself, but things with Zoey.

I didn't think there was any fixing it.

Apparently, it was like I had called to her.

I heard a rustling in the doorway, and I looked up. Zoey stood there, her blond hair flowing around her shoulders, her champagne-colored dress fitting her curves in a way that made me want to hold her.

She was stunning, the most beautiful woman I had ever seen.

And I had broken her heart.

As she looked at me, worry in her gaze, I didn't know how I was going to get her back.

Because I knew that, no matter what, I didn't deserve her.

I never had, and I didn't think I ever would.

Chapter 17

Zoey

I STOOD IN THE DOORWAY, MY WHOLE BODY SHAKING, AND I hoped I looked like I was sane, that I had the strength I needed. Because I certainly didn't feel like I did.

Caleb lay there in a hospital bed, machines hooked to him, an IV in his arm. He looked so different. Scared? Worried? Exhausted? I had seen some of the signs before. But when I'd asked…he'd lied to me.

Lied.

"Why didn't you tell me?"

I hadn't meant those words to be the first thing out of my mouth, but I couldn't help it. I should have asked how he was, what the plan was. But, no, he'd hurt me, and I needed to know *why*. The fact that Amelia had already filled me in on the other details just made my pain more real.

Because Caleb would clearly rather push me away, lying and making me feel like I was worthless, rather than tell me the truth. I didn't know if I could come back from that. Because as I looked at him now, I saw the boy he had been, the man I had loved since I was eight. And I didn't know how to fix this.

How could I put those two images together—the boy he had been who'd evolved into the caring man I knew, with the man who had broken me?

"I don't know," he said, and he let out a sigh. "Can you come in? I'd like to talk to you."

"Now? You want to talk now." I smiled, but there was nothing happy about it. I didn't want to be bitter, though. This wasn't me. And I couldn't let this change me more than it already had. This was our first true fight, and I didn't know if it was going to be our last.

Because he was in a hospital bed, I took the few steps into the room and closed the door behind me.

"I really shouldn't be here. You need some sleep."

"No, don't go."

"Your sister called me and told me what happened."

He swallowed hard. "She told you everything?"

"About the doctor visits, why you moved here, every-thing. It's something *you* should've done. We were together for how long? And even if it was just a pity fuck the entire time, I deserve better than that."

I wasn't crying, *I was angry*.

At my use of crude language, Caleb's eyes widened. "Jesus, Zoey. You were never a pity fuck."

"But that's what you made me feel like today. By bringing *her*."

"Christy's just a friend. I told you that. And she knew that going in."

"Yes, I actually met her." His eyes went wide. He looked comical, and I let out a rueful laugh. "Yes, she came up to me to make sure that I knew that she wasn't poaching. That she had only come to make sure you knew what a great girl I was or some crap like that. And the thing is? Just like with every other woman I've met who's been with you, I couldn't hate her."

"What are you talking about?"

I shook my head, a smile playing on my lips at my own naivety. "I couldn't hate her because you didn't treat her poorly. And she walked away happy. Even if she couldn't have you, she was still happy in the end. I've never understood that. How you could go through so many women throughout your life, and they could all walk away knowing that they had a part of you. Still feeling fulfilled in the end."

"Zoey."

"I'm not done yet."

"You're right." He closed his mouth, studying me. What would he see? The remains of the woman who had loved him? The scorned woman who felt as if she could burn this place to the ground?

Or Zoey. Hopeless. Lost. And *here*.

"Every time I saw you outside of our group of friends, you were always with another woman. Even when we were eight and in Hawaii with that little girl that pushed me into the water by accident, you were still with another woman."

"I was eight, and she wasn't my girlfriend."

"You gave her your last piece of gum. That is like a vow of marriage when you're eight."

"Zoey."

"I'm just saying. Every time. Every state. Every long-distance meeting. At the campsite, at college."

"I don't want to talk about college."

"Tough shit. Because we're going to. I've always had a crush on you, Caleb. And I know part of you has always known that."

He didn't say anything, but I saw the answers in his eyes.

I let out a breath and started to pace. "And I don't even know why I'm baring myself to you right now, but I guess I'm kind of tired of hiding things. Maybe like you're tired of hiding the fact that you're sick. But, no, you didn't tell me that. You had to pass out at my sister's wedding." I held up a hand as he almost started to speak again. "But I digress. I'll get back to that in a minute. You hurt me, Caleb. You hurt me using someone from your past. And, yes, you said it was platonic, just friends, and I truly believe that. Because I don't think you're that cruel. I don't think you would actually cheat on me. But you still did something in the vague vicinity of infidelity. And part of me is angry at myself for even letting it get this far."

"None of this is on you," he said quickly.

"Part of it is. I should have asked for labels. I should have said that we were exclusive. Because we never put those parameters on our relationship. So, I honestly can't get angry about that."

"Yeah, you can. I was an asshole."

"I'm glad we both agree on that." I smiled ruefully. "Anyway, I can get over Christy. Because I like her." I let out a laugh. "Just like I liked every single other woman who's ever been in your life. Because they're amazing women, and you have great taste. But I don't think I can get over the fact that you didn't tell me you were sick. I asked you point-blank if you were feeling okay several times, and you said, '*oh, it's just a headache.*' But you had migraines. To the point where you're in a hospital right now and waiting on test results. Migraines that made you move from Alaska to Colorado. And you never told me. Why? Why did you feel that you couldn't trust me with this information? You told your family, but you didn't tell me. The woman you're sleeping with. The person you spend most of your time with. That tells me that I was nothing more than just a warm body in a bed for you. Because you needed to tell me that. You should have. And I don't know what to do about the fact that you couldn't and didn't." Tears fell freely down my cheeks, and Caleb moved, trying to get closer.

A nurse walked in with a frown. "Your vitals are up. Don't bother him, miss."

"It's fine," Caleb said gruffly. "I'm fine. Leave us alone, okay?"

The nurse raised a brow.

I turned. "I'm almost done, I'm sorry. I'll try to be calm."

"And I didn't mean to be rude. I apologize. I'm a bastard. I know it. We just need a minute."

The nurse looked at both of us, gave us a tight nod, and then walked away.

"I don't know how to explain it other than I was scared."

I looked at him then, surprised. "What?" I said.

"I was scared," he repeated. "I didn't tell my brothers or Amelia until well after I had moved back here. I was scared because I didn't know what was happening. I had a hallucination in Alaska, Zoey. Saw things that weren't there. And I was afraid. I couldn't work in my old job, couldn't trust myself, so I came here. Now, I work behind a fucking desk because I was scared. And, yeah, I like my job now, but I changed everything in my life because I didn't have the answers. And I was too chickenshit to do anything about it."

I wanted to reach out and hold him, to tell him that everything was going to be okay, but I held myself back. I didn't know if I could hold him, and frankly, I didn't know if I had that right anymore. If I ever had. "I just really wish you would've told me. And I guess it's selfish of me to want to know more about you, but because you used it against me, it feels a little personal."

"I only did all of that so you wouldn't be hurt."

I blinked. "Excuse me?"

"I wasn't thinking clearly, and I know it makes no sense. But like…what if it was a tumor? I didn't want you to have to date a guy that could die."

I just looked at him, aghast. "You shut up right now. You don't get to make those choices for me."

"I didn't mean to. I just didn't know how to tell you. What to tell you. Because I didn't have any answers. I mean, I knew I needed to open up, but I didn't want to until I had an actual battle plan and answers. You know?"

"Maybe. I don't know, Caleb." I started to pace, the gold of my dress swishing under the harsh hospital lights.

"I had it in my head that once I had answers, things would be okay. That I would be able to fix it and would be able to talk it over with you. It was like this block in my head, and I couldn't stop keeping it a secret. It made no sense. But I am sorry. I was just scared."

I moved forward, swallowing hard. I was so close then that I reached out, trailing my fingertips across his hand. He gripped my fingers, squeezing tightly. It startled me.

"I'm sorry, Zoey. If I could go back and change it all, I would. I would tell you everything. Even if I was scared. Because I wanted to. I really did. I just couldn't."

"You didn't," I corrected.

"And I guess, I don't know, I don't even know how we started dating," he said, and I took a step back. He held on to my hand, though. I couldn't move. "That's not what I meant."

"Please explain to me exactly what you did mean." I said the words very slowly; crisp and precise.

"All I know is that you've always been a part of my life. And then somehow you were a different part, and I didn't know how or when exactly that happened. All I knew was that I really liked it. I liked you being in my life. I liked the fact that I had you there. Not only was the sex amazing—because it is," he said, and I laughed despite myself. "God, I love that laugh."

"Don't," I warned, sobering instantly.

"You're right. Hell, if I could get down on my knees right now and grovel, I would, but I really don't have the energy."

"You don't have to get on your knees to grovel," I muttered.

He smiled then, and it went right to my heart.

Stupid heart.

"I made so many mistakes. And not telling you exactly what I feel, and what was going on with me is probably the biggest one. But I kept things casual. I even told you that. I needed to keep things that particular way because I wasn't sure what the future would hold. I'm still not a hundred percent sure, but it doesn't look as grey or as dark as it did."

"I'm not very good at casual," I blurted.

"I know. You're in the business of love and romance, and you deserve something more than casual, but you were never a pity fuck."

"Well, never make me feel like one again."

"Does that mean you'll take me back?"

I shrugged, my heart racing, and my head pounding. "I don't know. Because what if something else happens and you run away again? What if you hide important things from me because you're too scared to talk about them? I'm supposed to be your partner. That's what a relationship is. And if I can't trust you to tell me the scary things, then how can I trust you with anything else? How can I trust you with me? My heart?"

He leaned forward and ran his hand over my arm. It was the only part I let him reach. "I'm going to try and do better. Because I never want to make you feel that way again. I was scared, and I admit that freely. I'm not a man who admits those kinds of things."

"I know."

Caleb was always strong, the fierce protector who lurked in the background. He'd always been with his family, even back when things weren't great between them all. So, having him admit that vulnerability was a deep thing. I just hated that I had gotten hurt because of it.

"I want to fix this," Caleb said. "Tell me how."

"You have to talk to me. You have to tell me things."

"I will. I promise. Just like I'm going to tell my family. Hell, I've got to be better at this."

"You really do." There was a pause as I tried to figure out what I wanted to do, what I wanted to say. I was so worried that I was going to say the wrong thing. Or that he wasn't going to say anything at all.

"You love me?" he asked, bringing me out of my thoughts. I froze.

"You remember that?"

"Of course, I do. You said you loved me."

"Just don't throw it in my face. Because it's bad

enough that we have all the same friends, and your family is so close to me now. I just…I can't. Because I've loved you forever, you asshole."

He grinned then, and it finally reached his eyes. "I love you, too, Zoey-girl. And as soon as I can, as soon as I get out of this bed, I'm going to grovel on my knees and show you that I love you. Because I want you in my life, I want to figure out exactly how to be the kind of person who shares. And I want to be that person with you. You've been a part of my life for as long as I can remember. I don't want to lose you. I love you, Zoey-girl. Take me back. Forgive me. And tell me exactly what I need to do to earn your trust again."

While I didn't really have anything to say, I couldn't anyway because the tears were flowing freely.

This was the Caleb Carr I had fallen in love with. The Caleb I had always known was buried deep down inside. And as I leaned down and kissed his lips, I knew that I would forgive him, even if he did need to grovel a bit more.

Because I had loved him since I was eight, and through every incarnation of him in my life, I had loved his soul, his smile, just him. As he trailed his fingers down my cheek and whispered my name, I knew I had forgiven him already.

I had been scared before, too, and I had pushed others away because of it.

I understood.

And he would be mine. It was a promise I had made when I was little, and it was a promise I was finally going to keep.

I had written Caleb Carr on my heart years ago, and as he held me in that hospital room, and we looked towards the future that wouldn't be perfect but would be ours, I knew I would write it again and again.

Because I was shameless when it came to Caleb Carr.

And that was just fine with me.

Epilogue

Caleb

"I, CALEB, TAKE YOU ZOEY-GIRL, TO BE MY LAWFULLY wedded wife. To have and to hold. For richer or poorer. Until the day our souls meet again. I love you with every ounce of my being. I have loved you since long before I knew what love was. I'll cherish you until the end of our days, and long past that. I'll be yours forever, I promise."

The officiant cleared his throat, and I winked at him.

"Sorry, needed to add a few extras."

"That's just fine," the officiant said, smiling.

"And now, Zoey?"

My bride looked at me, her eyes wide, tears spilling down her cheeks as she squeezed my hands.

"I, Zoey, take you, Caleb, love of my life, to have and

to hold, for richer or poorer, until the end of our days and beyond. Because I love you. I've loved you since we were children and didn't understand exactly what could be. I have loved you since before I could have you, and ever since. I've loved you even when both of us were hard to love. Since you told me you loved me."

I swallowed hard, my eyes stinging.

"The rings," the officiant continued.

Dimitri handed me my ring, and I winked at my brother.

"Thanks."

"You've got this," Dimitri whispered.

"Now, take Zoey's hand and put the ring on her finger. And, I'm sure like we said before, you have your own vows for this."

"Zoey-girl," I said, swallowing hard again as I slid the ring on her finger. "With this ring, I thee wed. With this ring, I'm forever yours. With this ring, I promise you my devotion, my truth, and my secrets. I promise you…me."

There was open weeping from the front of the room, but I only had eyes for my soon-to-be wife.

She slipped the ring on my hand, saying the same words back to me, and when the officiant pronounced us husband and wife, I leaned down and gently trailed my fingers along her cheek.

"Are you ready, Zoey-girl?" I asked.

"I've been waiting for you forever, Caleb Carr."

"And now you have me, *Zoey Carr.*"

She beamed, and then I lowered my mouth to hers, dipped her down, and then kissed her. My wife. I couldn't fucking wait to see what happened next.

"WELL, there wasn't a dry eye in the house," Dimitri said, holding his son Kane as the child slept.

The baby was almost a year old now, but it was still our first baby of the family.

"We try," I said dryly, taking a sip of my champagne.

I looked towards the dance floor as one of the Montgomerys spun my wife around, her laugh reaching my ears and making me grin.

"Jesus Christ, that's my wife," I said.

"Hey, I think I shared that exact same sentiment when I looked at Thea for the first time. And watch your language around my son."

I looked down at the sleeping Kane and grinned.

"With both of the kid's extended families, you're out of luck there when it comes to language."

Dimitri winced. "Pretty much."

"Oh, can I hold the baby?" Erin said, waddling over.

She was newly into her second trimester, but with twins, she had gotten bigger quicker than anyone expected.

But I would never actually tell her that.

"You can nuzzle him, but you know my brother will hurt me if I give you a sleeping baby while you're not supposed to be holding anything."

"I'm having twins, I'm fine," she said, but she slid her fingers down Kane's nose, grinning as the baby made cooing sounds in his sleep.

"Seriously, that's got to be the cutest baby."

"He really is," Amelia said as she came up with Tucker. Her hand was on the small mound of her belly, and I just shook my head. Dimitri and Thea had the one baby, Erin and Devin were on their way to having two. But was that enough? No, baby Amelia Carr had to have *three*.

Yes, Amelia was pregnant with triplets. So, with their son Evan, who was on the dance floor with Thea, they would have a family of six, with room for Evan's mom and dad whenever they stayed over.

We were all a huge group, a family tighter than we'd ever been before.

And we were doing fine.

I was on good meds, and I took care of myself better than I ever had. I loved my job, and I had my wife.

I didn't need anything else, really.

Zoey looked over at me and winked, and I prowled over to her, not even noticing when I pushed a Montgomery out of the way so I could hold her in my arms.

"You know, you're being a little grumbly."

"I can't help it. I just want to keep kissing you."

"Mmm, you taste like yummy champagne, and I wish I could have more."

"You will in eight months," I said and winked.

Lacey and John had indeed asked her to be their surrogate, but they were using a donor egg, rather than Zoey's for reasons of their own. The fact that Zoey had said yes, hadn't surprised me. She would do anything for her sister, and hell, I would do anything for the couple, as well. In a way, they had brought us together.

"Eventually, though, it'd be nice to do this for ourselves," Zoey said, winking.

"Yeah?"

"Sure, let's do that. You and me. In a couple of years? Let's see what beautiful babies we can make."

I spun my wife out on the dance floor, looking over my shoulder at my family, who all hung around the children, knowing that there would be more babies to come. And soon.

I looked at the gorgeous woman in my arms. She was my Zoey-girl—my past, my present, and my future.

And I would likely kick myself to the end of my days for wasting so much time, spending so much of my life without her. But now she was mine, just like I was hers.

And I couldn't wait to travel the world with her and have her be my girl from now until forever.

THE END

The Carrs and the Less Than series might be over, but they might show up in the other Montgomery World novels!

WANT TO READ A SPECIAL BONUS EPILOGUE FEATURING ZOEY AND CALEB? CLICK HERE

A Note from Carrie Ann Ryan

Thank you so much for reading **SHAMELESS WITH HIM.** I do hope if you liked this story, that you would please leave a review!

This book might be my favorite of the series because the two just fell into each other. Fun story! The first chapter (and the bonus epilogue) are almost based in real life events. Almost. Except the HEA. However, there was a boy I met in random countries for YEARS until I was about sixteen. So when you ask where authors get their ideas, you just never know!

This might be the end of the Less Than series, but not the end of the Montgomery World!

And if you're new to my books, you can start anywhere within the my interconnected series and catch up! Each book is a stand alone, so jump around!

Don't miss out on the Montgomery Ink World!

- Montgomery Ink (The Denver Montgomerys)
- Montgomery Ink: Colorado Springs (The Colorado Springs Montgomery Cousins)
- Montgomery Ink: Boulder (The Boulder Montgomery Cousins)
- Gallagher Brothers (Jake's Brothers from Ink Enduring)
- Whiskey and Lies (Tabby's Brothers from Ink Exposed)
- Fractured Connections (Mace's sisters from Fallen Ink)
- Less Than (Dimitri's siblings from Restless Ink)
- Promise Me (Arden's siblings from Wrapped in Ink)

If you want to make sure you know what's coming next from me, you can sign up for my newsletter at www. CarrieAnnRyan.com; follow me on twitter at @Carrie-AnnRyan, or like my Facebook page. I also have a Facebook Fan Club where we have trivia, chats, and other goodies. You guys are the reason I get to do what I do and I thank you.

Make sure you're signed up for my MAILING LIST

so you can know when the next releases are available as well as find giveaways and FREE READS.

Happy Reading!

The Less Than Series:
Book 1: Breathless With Her
Book 2: Reckless With You
Book 3: Shameless With Him

Want to read a special **BONUS EPILOGUE** featuring Zoey and Caleb? **CLICK HERE**

About the Author

Carrie Ann Ryan is the New York Times and USA Today bestselling author of contemporary, paranormal, and young adult romance. Her works include the Montgomery Ink, Redwood Pack, Fractured Connections, and Elements of Five series, which have sold over 3.0 million books worldwide. She started writing while in graduate school for her advanced degree in chemistry and hasn't stopped since. Carrie Ann has written over seventy-five novels and novellas with more in the works. When she's not losing herself in her emotional and action-packed worlds, she's reading as much as she can while wrangling her clowder of cats who have more followers than she does.

www.CarrieAnnRyan.com

Also from Carrie Ann Ryan

The Montgomery Ink: Boulder Series:

Book 1: Wrapped in Ink

Book 2: Sated in Ink

Book 3: Embraced in Ink

Book 4: Seduced in Ink

Book 4.5: Captured in Ink

The Montgomery Ink: Fort Collins Series:

Book 1: Inked Persuasion

The Less Than Series:

Book 1: Breathless With Her

Book 2: Reckless With You

Book 3: Shameless With Him

The Elements of Five Series:

Book 1: From Breath and Ruin

Book 2: From Flame and Ash

Book 3: From Spirit and Binding

Book 4: From Shadow and Silence

The Promise Me Series:

Book 1: Forever Only Once

Book 2: From That Moment

Book 3: Far From Destined

Book 4: From Our First

The Fractured Connections Series:

Book 1: Breaking Without You

Book 2: Shouldn't Have You

Book 3: Falling With You

Book 4: Taken With You

Montgomery Ink: Colorado Springs

Book 1: Fallen Ink

Book 2: Restless Ink

Book 2.5: Ashes to Ink

Book 3: Jagged Ink

Book 3.5: Ink by Numbers

Montgomery Ink:

Book 0.5: Ink Inspired
Book 0.6: Ink Reunited
Book 1: Delicate Ink
Book 1.5: Forever Ink
Book 2: Tempting Boundaries
Book 3: Harder than Words
Book 4: Written in Ink
Book 4.5: Hidden Ink
Book 5: Ink Enduring
Book 6: Ink Exposed
Book 6.5: Adoring Ink
Book 6.6: Love, Honor, & Ink
Book 7: Inked Expressions
Book 7.3: Dropout
Book 7.5: Executive Ink
Book 8: Inked Memories
Book 8.5: Inked Nights
Book 8.7: Second Chance Ink

The Gallagher Brothers Series:
Book 1: Love Restored
Book 2: Passion Restored
Book 3: Hope Restored

The Whiskey and Lies Series:
Book 1: Whiskey Secrets

Book 7.7: The Hunted Heart
Book 8: Wicked Wolf

The Branded Pack Series:
(Written with Alexandra Ivy)
Book 1: Stolen and Forgiven
Book 2: Abandoned and Unseen
Book 3: Buried and Shadowed

Dante's Circle Series:
Book 1: Dust of My Wings
Book 2: Her Warriors' Three Wishes
Book 3: An Unlucky Moon
Book 3.5: His Choice
Book 4: Tangled Innocence
Book 5: Fierce Enchantment
Book 6: An Immortal's Song
Book 7: Prowled Darkness
Book 8: Dante's Circle Reborn

Holiday, Montana Series:
Book 1: Charmed Spirits
Book 2: Santa's Executive
Book 3: Finding Abigail
Book 4: Her Lucky Love
Book 5: Dreams of Ivory

The Happy Ever After Series:
Flame and Ink
Ink Ever After

Single Title:
Finally Found You